DBROCKMAN PUBLISHING PRESENTS:

COINCIDENTALLY MISHAPPENED

A BOOK OF SHORT STORIES: THE ANTHOLOGY

dbrockman publishing

Unless listed otherwise, Stories were edited by Torey William
Contact him at: twilli28@tampabay.rr.com
Dad's Advice was edited by Tammeaka Graham
Room 324, 423, & 212 were edited by Robert Cain

Art Illustration on cover was provided by
R. Burger of Custom Poster Work Inc. Orlando, Fl.
Contact him at: bob@customposterworks.com or (321) 206-9320
Picture can also be view at shutterfreaks.com

Mishappened, Coincidences

ISBN 978-0-9787439-1-8 0

Publisher By:
DBROCKMAN PUBLISHING,
Post Office Box 173208
Tampa, Florida 33672
Local Phone (813) 390-1556
Info@dbrockmansr.info
dbpublisher@yahoo.com

dbrockman publishing

Prefix

Acknowledgement Page

First I would like to thank the Almighty, God, which lives in me and He sent His son to die for my sins. I would like to thank everyone who participated for without your short stories there would not have been a project called "Anthology".

Padget Williams: My Earthly Angel who also just blessed me with a Little Angel. Thank you for the story, and I can't wait to publish more of your work. Thanks for breathing the life of writing into me, for that I will forever be grateful.

Bob Cain: Your work is ingenious. It's an honor to have a piece of your work published under my name. I will never forget the "plenty of talks" we had about the Market Street Apartments. You are the next Steven King, write on!

Jamie Bush: It takes a 'BIG' man to share with the world what you have shared with me. I got very emotional the first time I read your story, but sometimes we have to lose something to appreciate other things. Thanks for the write!

Tammeaka Graham: After reading your story I couldn't get it out of my head for weeks, it was like looking at a really good suspense movie with a twist at the end. Through my eyes, your writing is immaculate and you really need to write more. Thanks for the story.

I would like to thank everyone who devoted time into this project. I don't have to worry about the project succeeding because it was a success just working with you all. Thanks for the commitment!

Table of Contents

PUBLISHING INFORMATION
PREFIX

ACKNOWLEDGEMENTS
Pg i

THE PROLOGUE
Pg 3

MORALS
Pg 6

STELLA-MAE'S WALK TO LIBERTY
Pg 12

ROOM 324
Pg 18

LOVE NOT TO LOVE
Pg 30

DEATH IS ONLY THE BEGINNING
Pg 40

ROOM 423
Pg 50

TYPICAL SUNDAY
Pg 60

DAD'S ADVICE
Pg 64

TOUGH LOVE
Pg 94

ROOM *212*
Pg 108

THE WRAP-UP
Pg 128

EARLY – MID 80's
PG 130

MID 80's – EARLY 90's
PG 138

THE MISHAPPENED
PG 144

THE COINCIDENCE
PG 149

THE PROMISE
PG 151

COINCIDENTALLY MISHAPPENED

A BOOK OF SHORT STORIES:
THE ANTHOLOGY

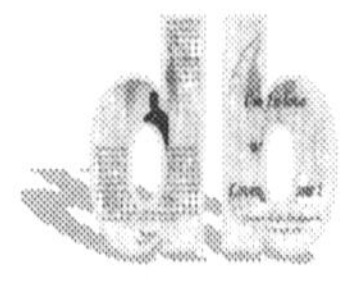

A Book of Short Stories: The Anthology

Coincidentally Mishappened

MORALS
A SHORT STORY BY DEXTER BROCKMAN SR.

The Prologue

Have you ever searched for someone for more than ten years just to end up bumping into him or her while walking down the isle of the grocery store? Have you ever received a phone call or an e-mail from a person that you were just thinking about a couple days ago? Isn't that just a coincidence that you had that person on your mind and you regained contact with them...Or is it?

Have you ever been driving along the Interstate and needed to get off on the next exit, but the car beside you wouldn't let you get over? After you exit off at the next exit and loop back around to reach your original goal you notice a massive accident where a truck driver fell asleep at the wheel, crushing and killing everyone in the car it hit. It freaks you out to discover that the car that was

MORALS
A SHORT STORY BY DEXTER BROCKMAN SR.

crushed was the same car that wouldn't let you get over so you could've gotten off on the right exit. Was that just a mishappened event, or was the accident meant for you but coincidentally you somehow missed it?

All of these stories pertain to mishappened events that have coincidentally taken place in many different places and at many different times. Some people don't believe in coincidence, they would say its fate. Then there are some people who question things that mishappen, believing if it's meant to be that your paths will meet.

For me, I can't say one way or the other. I can only ensure the readers that all of these events Coincidentally Mishappened!

MORALS
A SHORT STORY BY DEXTER BROCKMAN SR.

pg 5

DBrockman Publishing Presents:

Moral's

A Short Story By: DBrockman Sr

MORALS
A SHORT STORY BY DEXTER BROCKMAN SR.

One gloomy day an eager young man (Sebastian) apprehended a journey aside his niche to a town that was just on the other side of the bridge. The day was growing old and he wanted to make it back home so he could watch the *GOLD* disappear (the sun set). Upon crossing the bridge he saw some weight lifting gloves that were attached to two weight bars. He stopped to try on the first glove, it fit perfectly. The young man ventured to the end of the bridge to make sure no one was around, then retreated back to gather the other glove. He placed the glove upon his hand and proceeded toward the town. As he journeyed he passed a house with an open door. The gentleman (Ramon) in the house notices the gloves on Sebastian's hands and questions him. Sebastian begins to put some pep into stride as Ramon filters his voice with anger yelling, "Hey, Hey...Those are my gloves!" Sebastian ran behind the house, attempting to hide from Ramon, but the well-lit area failed to hide him. Ramon spotted Sebastian and started to approach him, but Sebastian sees him coming and flees the city while Ramon continuously yells for him to halt. Sebastian ran through numerous yards, jumping from one porch to another. Ramon turned back toward his house with a sigh and a slight grin upon his face as Sebastian vanished into the

MORALS
A SHORT STORY BY DEXTER BROCKMAN SR.

bushes.

Sebastian was forced to take a path less traveled, a road that he had no knowledge of where it would take him. His eyes were big, his mouth was dry and his blood vessels were filled with anxiety. All he could think about was getting into the clear so he could find a good hiding place. He ran into an apartment building where he passed a little boy (Dee) and a little Girl (Kera) playing on the steps. He raced up the stairs to the top floor. His heart was beating abnormally from the mere thought of what could happen to him if he was captured. When he approached the top floor he found a window that was visible to the street and also visible to the entrance of the building. He rested at the window, assuring that no one was entering the building without him knowing.

Moments passed...A door opened and a young lady (Tabula) stepped into the hall. Sebastian spotted her and instantly began to communicate. He explained his reason for being in the building while he walked her to the stairs. He heard the entrance door of the building open, but being that his interest was captured by the intriguing vocals this specimen placed in his ears he was not focused and not attentive to the voices of the two men approaching. He walked downstairs, spotted the two men

MORALS
A SHORT STORY BY DEXTER BROCKMAN SR.

walking away and sat beside Dee and Kera while pulling his hat over his face. He was afraid to make any sudden moves thinking the two men would see him. Then he heard one of the men singing a phrase from a song "Whatever you're doing, wherever you're at, when night falls from day nothing gold can stay..." Swiftly the two men turn to him and he notices that he was spotted. Off the steps he ran and out the door racing into the busy streets. He was jumping over cars while people were hitting on breaks, honking their horns and yelling out of their windows. Through his peripheral he saw a white El Dorado coming towards him. He quickly ran towards the sidewalk where the car followed him, hitting a fruit stand damaging the two owners of the stand.

Sebastian ran to the other side of the street looking back to see where the two men were. One of the men had on a white vest (Kenny) got out of the car and chased Sebastian down the busy street, but Sebastian was much faster than the two gentlemen. Sebastian turns a corner and ran through an alley that approached two condemned buildings. He stopped between them to catch his breath and to gather himself. He chose to go into the building on the right, where he saw two homeless women talking about what they had when they were young. He listens to

MORALS
A SHORT STORY BY DEXTER BROCKMAN SR.

them with sympathy, hoping his life never take a turn that will force him to live in abandoned buildings. He sat with the women and explained his troubles and asked for their advice. Before they could reply they heard a noise in the building across from them. They peeped out the window and saw the two men. They notified Sebastian and rushed him to the loft where they hide when trouble approaches. Minutes later the two men entered the building. They questioned the women about Sebastian. Sebastian could barely hear for the pounding thumps of his heartbeat and his blood racing through his veins. He was in an uncomfortable position and decided to move for comfort. When he stretched his leg he turned over a can, giving away his position. He heard the two men asking the women "What was that?", but they denied they heard anything. The men started toward the loft where Sebastian was hiding. The women yelled, "Run they're coming!" Sebastian pushed the door and as it sprung open he swiftly leaped from the loft. He then climbed out of a nearby window where Kenny followed his every move. Sebastian jumped a fence and onto a gravel road. While he was looking for somewhere to hide he heard the men singing the song "Whatever you're doing, wherever you're at, when night falls from day nothing gold can stay". He

MORALS
A SHORT STORY BY DEXTER BROCKMAN SR.

crawled on his knees and hid in a bush hoping the men would have thought he ran down the unpaved road. The singing began to get louder as if they knew where he was hiding. He peeps from around the bush to see if he was in the clear. There he saw Kenny halfway over the fence pointing in the direction where he was hiding. Ramon got tired of the chase pulled out his gun and started shooting. Sebastian curled up in a ball hoping not to get hit. After a while he didn't hear any more gunshots, but he heard a loud thump and police sirens.

Sebastian waited a few minutes before he departed the bushes. He spotted blood on the fence. He jumped back over the fence where he saw Kenny laying in a puddle of blood. He ran back to the building to look for the two women. He saw a gun lying on the floor but no one was there. He looked out of the building window that was visible to the street. He saw police cars coming from afar and he saw Ramon sitting on the ground with his arms wrapped around his legs and his head buried in his knees. Sebastian approached Ramon and asked him softly "What's the Opportunity Cost?" as he placed the gloves beside him and disappeared in the GOLD.

DBROCKMAN PUBLISHING PRESENTS:

STELLA-MAE'S WALK TO LIBERTY

A SHORT STORY BY: PADGET WILLIAMS

COINCIDENTALLY MISHAPPENED
THE ANTHOLOGY
STELLA-MAE'S WALK TO LIBERTY
A SHORT STORY BY PADGET WILLIAMS

"Stella-Mae, Stella-Mae, you hear me calling you, get me some cold water". Luther screamed from the bedroom. Stella-Mae was in the bathroom trying to pull her self together. They had another knock down drag out episode and as usual Luther won. Stella-Mae was holding a cold washcloth on the bump on her forehead she must have hit the footboard of the bed when Luther flung her across the room. It all happened so fast that she could not get any clear comprehension of the whole event.

Stella-Mae emerged from the bathroom and walked to the kitchen to get Luther some water as she made her way down the long hallway she thought, "how will I ever get away from this man"? How did I end up here"? The questions just kept coming, She remembered the man she fell in love with, the Luther that sang to her, the romantic man who wined and dined her. But shortly after he lost his job and the custody of his kids because of his drinking, all he was interested in was getting drunk and fighting. Stella-Mae stuck by him through it all but, how soon he forgot how supportive she had been. When he was inconsolable in the courtroom she held his hand, when he was too depressed to look for a job, she took a job cleaning offices at night. She did everything she could to help him, but without a high school education she never made enough money to support a household of 7 people. Luther's growl drowned out her thoughts. "Stella-Mae, bring me a beer along with the water". Stella-Mae reached the kitchen and poured some ice water in a glass and drank without a pause, and then she poured another glass and grabbed a beer from the bottom shelf.

"Here you go Luther" Stella-Mae said. Luther just reached out for the beverages without a thank you. When Stella-Mae turned to leave he grabbed her by the night gown and said, "turn on the T.V. on your way out and take a shower while you're at it, you stink!" Stella-Mae had just pushed the power button on the television when she felt a sharp pain in her back then she heard Luther say "and brush your hair, you look like crap" the brush Luther threw had hit Stella-Mae right in the back, then it hit the floor. Luther just laughed and laughed like that was the funniest thing he ever saw. Stella-Mae felt like every thing was moving in slow motion. Out of sheer reflex Stella-Mae picked up Luther's precious bowling trophy (old school style made of metal) and threw it as hard as she could it hit Luther straight in the face.

When Stella-Mae realized what she had done Luther was coming at her in full force blood running from his nose, he was screaming and cursing I'm gonna kill you, you lost your mind, look what you did. Stella-Mae tried to get out of the room but Luther was too close, he grabbed Stella-Mae's arm and began to twist it behind her back while blood was still pouring down his face. She screamed, "please Luther stop, stop you going to break my arm." Luther was so in raged he did not hear her pleading for him to let go. "See what you did!" He pushed her to the floor and sat on her back with her arm still in that twisted position.

Stella-Mae could not free her arm and the pain was unbearable as if that was not enough Luther started slapping her in the back of the head with both hands. He worked himself into frenzy; she could feel sweat falling on her and just when she was about to pass out from the pain Luther fell over on to the floor. She waited a few minutes before moving just in case he was just taking a

Stella-Mae's Walk to Liberty
A Short Story by Padget Williams

break, when he didn't move she looked over at him and saw foam coming from his mouth and he had started to shake uncontrollably.

Stella-Mae had never seen him like this before. She went to the phone and called 911. The police and the paramedics were dispatched. They checked Stella-Mae and got Luther stable enough to be transported to the hospital.

The police told Stella-Mae, "When the doctor's release him he will be going to jail."

They asked Stella-Mae if she would like to remain in the home or if she wanted a ride to the battered women's shelter?

She replied, "I'll walk its right down the street." So with her arm in a sling and a small bag of clothes Stella-Mae walked down the street with peace in her heart she finally got away older, but much wiser!

Room 324
A Short Story by Bob Cain

DBROCKMAN PUBLISHING PRESENTS:

ROOM 324

A SHORT STORY BY: BOB CAIN

Room 324
A Short Story by Bob Cain

It was a dark and stormy night. Of course, that was there, on the black and white TV in the bedroom, next to the picture of his mother and the bottle of Jade East she had given him at Christmas in 1968. This evening, outside the Market Street Apartments, the moon smiled down from the cloudless sky. Nothing was happening and Kevin was bored.

It is currently 2am, and as far estranged from any other Saturday 2am Kevin ever knew. Usually from his room on the corner of the third floor, he could peer down and see the steady flow of customers going in and out of Voelker's Bar. During early morning, too, there would often come a calling on his curtains the flashing red and white lights of a friendly police car, as the friendly police officers were summoned to break up a fight or to smooth over a sick lovers dispute. Sometimes it was worse, but not tonight, and Kevin was very sad.

He rolled the wheelchair closer to the window and gazed longingly down to the black street, which offered no relief from the lethargic monotony which sought to consume him. Then turning back toward the crackling TV screen, he rolled across the floor and poked the power button which sent it and the room spiraling downward

ROOM 324
A SHORT STORY BY BOB CAIN

into an all-too-familiar, silent abyss of tedium and cruel darkness. Yes, he was sad.

"You know, Mother, I never thought I'd be this so unhappy," he said, gazing at her picture and remembering how it had been when she was alive. "Here we are."

Kevin rolled over to the window, again. Something had to happen. It was just too quiet, **too perfect**, he thought. He pushed the curtain slowly aside. In the distance a car turned onto 1st Avenue, its taillights waving a red farewell.

He remembered the accident, again. Mother was driving and the snow had covered the icy streets with a sort of deadly powdered sugar tinged with arsenic. Mother was angry this time. She had just left her lover's apartment where Kevin had supposed she had found her lover with another girl. Mother was angry and silent. She had expected to be paid something for being so very kind to this guy while he was unemployed; but instead, after he found a job and finally got paid, there had been yelling, a smashing of glass and a hasty retreat. Mom pressed the gas pedal down and never once let up on it as we sailed silently out of Wisconsin.

ROOM 324
A SHORT STORY BY BOB CAIN

Kevin closed his eyes. "You always drove too fast, Mother," he said, remembering the sounds as they lost control of the car as it flew over the shoulder into some farmer's grove north of Zion. He remembered waking up in Zion Memorial Hospital unable to move for months as he replayed the doctor's words that he would never walk again -- the first prognoses which cursed him to his chair. He opened his eyes.

Suddenly there was movement on the street below. A woman was slowly walking down the opposite side of the street toward him. He looked closer. It was strange but didn't she surely look so much like Mother. He noticed her cheeks were shiny as if she had been crying. And he watched her as she paused underneath the 1st Avenue and Market Street corner streetlight, removed a handkerchief from her purse and ran it over her eyes.

Tears . . . it must be tears, he thought. **I wonder why?** He pushed the window open so he could hear her footfalls as she walked by like he was a patron at a private one act play. She came closer, walking, stopping, walking again. She crossed 1st and soon she was directly across from his window. He could see the smeared mascara had etched a rune-like message on her cheeks. It said she had

ROOM 324
A SHORT STORY BY BOB CAIN

been hurt by a world not even the paralyzed could never know.   As she sat down in the doorway of Weirton Hardware and cried into her hands. Kevin detected the glint of a sequined glow emanating from beneath her raincoat. **Yes, she must be a dancer at one of the wild clubs near 4th Avenue, and she is now just returning home**, he thought.

She reached into her purse and found the gun. The burnished silver of the Walther shot a ray of reflected streetlight into Kevin's eyes. She lifted the gun slowly to her chest and cried again. Then, gathering herself as an actress might before her final curtain, she slowly lifted her head and gazed directly across the street and into the 3rd story window at the face of a man she had never seen before. What?! Was he watching her?

"You!" she said while she put the gun in purse. "What the hell are you staring at?"

As she stood up and adjusted her coat, Kevin backed away from the open window. Her voice dripped like honey. It was like one he had heard once long ago singing a lullaby.

"I know you're there," she said matter-of-factly. "Ain't no use tryin' to hide. What did you expect to see? A

ROOM 324
A SHORT STORY BY BOB CAIN

suicide?!" Her voice rose slowly as she crossed the street. "Hey, you at the window, weren't you even gonna try 'n stop me?"

Kevin shook in his chair. He knew she was right. He wasn't going to stop her. Just as he sat by and watched other people waiting outside the bar next door, just as he watched them spring out from the alleyway to plant the hilts of their knives into the bellies and backs of others, Kevin <u>never</u> said anything. As far as he was concerned, the world was made up of cause and effect. And if asked him he would say it was not his place to interfere with the destiny of others.

"Hey, you! Talk to me!" She yelled from the alleyway this time. Kevin came closer to the window and saw the lady disappear below. Then he heard the sound of the fire escape ladder being pulled down. **Oh my God, she was coming to visit him.**

He quickly slammed shut and locked all the windows, drew the drapes and retreated to a far wall. "Mother, they have found me," he cried softly as a woman's shadow moved stealthily by the window. **I was a fool. I was a fool. Why didn't I just mind my own business? Why didn't I just go to sleep?** A dozen

ROOM 324
A SHORT STORY BY BOB CAIN

unanswered questions ran through his mind as the pane in the living room smashed inward and a delicate porcelain hand reached through to unlock the latch. As in slow motion, the window rose and the woman crawled in.

"I've got a g-gun." His voice quavered because it was always difficult for him to lie. "Get out or I'll sh-shoot."

She knew from the way he spoke he was lying. "Don't be silly, you don't have a gun." She stopped by the couch and hit her purse with the side of her hand. "I'm the one with the gun . . . remember?"

"What do you want? What do *you* want?"

"Calm down," she said condescendingly as she came closer and her eyes adjusted to the dark. "What's this?" She noticed the wheelchair. "Oh my my my. Well, well, it looks like I've gone and found myself a nice little crip. Now what ... will I do?" She paused as she spoke those words, hanging on the word "what" until she noticed a slight shutter from Kevin. She removed her Walther from the purse and sat with it beside her on his couch.

Kevin moaned. It was a moan of someone who had failed at everything in life – a deep guttural uttering of

**ROOM 324
A SHORT STORY BY BOB CAIN**

resignation. He slumped slightly forward and thought now would be a good time to pray.

"My name's Monte ... Monte Carlo Jones."

He didn't laugh as she went on.

"And I was just wondering. I wonder what kind of a person it is who would sit by an open window and watch somebody cry? Now I know, it's not much of a whole person after all, is it?" She got up, took the gun and walked to the refrigerator. She opened the door. "Let's see now. No bccr. It figures I'd find someone who doesn't drink. Shit. Seems to me if I was a crip, all I'd wanna do is drink." She closed the door and came back to the couch. "I should've guessed you weren't normal."

Kevin looked up. She was beautiful in a frightening sort of way. Not quite 25 as far as he could guess, her body was that of a dancer. She smiled through her smudged green eyes and for a moment touched something emerald in his aching heart. "What do you want?" he asked again, this time with a little more control, a sound more of concern than fear.

She looked at him not knowing exactly what to make of him now. Was this the tactic a creature takes when it's defeated? Was this a deliberate play for

ROOM 324
A SHORT STORY BY BOB CAIN

sympathy? No, he genuinely cared. And his look now was almost pathetic, if it hadn't have been so empathetic.

Monte knew he was defeated and she felt sad to have taken advantage of the situation by being so mean as to hurt someone she hardly knew. He was defeated, she had won, and now, because he cared, she let him know she did not really mean him harm.

She smiled and handed him the gun. "I don't mean to hurt you. Honest. Here, take this."

He took the gun and looked at it closely. It was loaded. He placed it on his lap and looked toward Monte for answers. "What happened to you?" he asked.

"Look, mister, ah what is your name anyway?"

"Kevin."

"Look, Kevin, I don't want to cause you no problem. I just lost my job. Dancer at the Flame on 5th. I wouldn't let the manager fuck around in the back room so he said 'walk.' I knew it wouldn't be so bad, you know, finding something else, but when I got home, my apartment was robbed. Took everything. My savings. Clothes. Everything. Even my dog. All I have is what I got on, damn it." She started to cry. "Not that I would expect any

Room 324
A Short Story by Bob Cain

sympathy from you, Kevin, but do you have any suggestions about what I should do now?"

"Pray," he said, lifting the gun and pointing it at her face. "Don't move a single muscle and pray."

She didn't move but she did speak. "Oh, great. And now you're going to just blow me the fuck away aren't you?" she said sarcastically.

"Yes, I am," he said, pressing slowly on the trigger.

"Wait. I have a son. He's at a friend's house. He needs me."

"Then you should have stayed at home with him! But you didn't, did you? No, you just went out running around and left him with someone who probably doesn't even care one bit about him."

"But, listen . . . he needs me," she cried.

"No, he doesn't, Monte. You're life is a mess and you are a mess."

Kevin pulled the trigger and a bullet cut away Monte's forehead. It was a clean shot grazing the temporal lobe. Monte fell forward and lifeless at his feet.

After his phone call to the police, Kevin unlocked the door and waited. Soon they arrived and the lights from the police car floated through the curtains like a

ROOM 324
A SHORT STORY BY BOB CAIN

Broadway show. Oh what a great morning it had become. He opened the door, the police were given a story about a robbery and the body was taken away. As the new day dawned, the police helped Kevin clean up the broken glass and put plastic over the broken window, all the time telling him over and over how lucky he had been to get the upper hand.

When they left, Kevin smiled as he got ready for bed. Just before he went to sleep, he turned on his side and gazed at the picture of his mother on the nightstand near the bottle of Jade East she had given to him in 1968.

"You know, Mother, that was pretty exciting, wasn't it? Of course it was. What? You want to know why I killed her? Oh, you're such a kidder, mother." Kevin giggled as he turned the picture of his mother over.

Suddenly his eyes became lifeless; suddenly his countenance became one of solemn, deep remorse. Kevin realized it was possible that there would never be another moment in his life as sublime and as perfect as this one. Furthermore, with the epiphany that this moment was probably not in anyway divinely inspired, Kevin was not smiling.

ROOM 324
A SHORT STORY BY BOB CAIN

"You, see, Mother, I had to kill her. She was so much like you." Kevin yawned and sighed as he rested his head on his pillow.

"What a bitch."

DBROCKMAN PUBLISHING PRESENTS:

LOVE NOT TO LOVE

A SHORT STORY BY: DBROCKMAN SR.

Coincidentally Mishappened
The Anthology

Love not to Love
A Short Story by Dexter Brockman Sr.

Drip, drip, drip, drippidy, drip was the sound of the rain hitting the top of the bus. It was a nasty day. The bus driver drove five miles under the speed limit because he could barely see the roads. As the bus came to a stop two young ladies entered, closing their umbrellas and rumbling through their purses looking for bus fare. The driver closed the door and proceeded to drive down the road. One of the women said out loud, "Girl I can't find my money, do you have any money?"

The other woman looked to her and said, "I only have my bus pass, I don't walk around with money."

The bus driver instantly stopped the bus, "Young lady if you don't have bus fare then you can't ride this bus!" The way he looked at the woman you could tell that he was serious.

"You mean to tell me that you're going to put my girl off the bus in all that bad weather? I know your mother raised you better than that!" the woman chanted as she continued rambling through her purse searching for change for bus fare.

"Well its like those sayings in the bible, if you don't work you don't eat."

"WHAT THE HELL THAT GOT TO DO WITH ANYTHING? You talking about throwing my girl off the bus in a thunder storm and all you can do is quote what is probably the only verse you know in the bible!"

"Look, if she don't have bus fare she got to get off this bus. Maybe the bus driver that comes in thirty minutes may have more compassion. If someone on this bus go back to the compound and tell my supervisor that I let another person ride my bus for free then I will be out of a job."

The other woman turned and started walking towards the steps. "And like I said...if I don't work me, my four kids and my wife won't..."

LOVE NOT TO LOVE
A SHORT STORY BY DEXTER BROCKMAN SR.

Before he could finish the woman cut him off, "That's a bunch bull shii…"

"Excuse me ladies I couldn't help it, I over heard your conversation you were having with the bus driver, and I think you ladies are giving the man a harder time than he deserves." As the gentleman spoke the women listened, or they pretend they were listening, but in actuality their focus was on the lump of money the guy had in his hand. He took out a five-dollar bill and handed it to the bus driver. "Here, this should cover their cost."

The guy was about five-foot five, one hundred and eighty-five pounds solid. He didn't look like he had any fat over his entire body he was all muscles. He had a baldhead and you could see he had a receding hairline, that's the reason he was sporting a clean shave. He looked like the hip-hop rapper DMX. The only difference? He had four open-faced golds in the top of his mouth.

The woman stepped back up the step and she gave the bus driver a dirty look. "You thought you were going to put me off the bus didn't you? That's alright though, my knight with four open-faces came to my rescue, SUCKA!" She stated in a sassy voice as she walked pass the bus driver rubbing her hand across the young man's white satin shirt.

The girl with the bus pass was too angry to even make a statement, she just gave him a funny look as she turned and walk towards the back of the bus.

The gentleman walked to the back of the bus and he introduced himself as he took his seat, "Hello ladies my name is Callow, but you but you can call me Cal."

The woman stood up swiftly to shake his hand, "My name is Stella, Stella-Mae, but you can call me anything you like." Stella was about five-foot three one hundred and twenty-five pounds. Her body was very appealing, well

Coincidentally Mishappened
The Anthology

Love not to Love
A Short Story by Dexter Brockman Sr.

proportionate to her weight and her height. But her arm was in a sling.

Cal extended his hand, "The pleasure is all mine." as he pulled her hand towards his lips.

"Oh look girl and he a gentleman, you may have hit the jackpot this time." the other woman expressed as she jumped up to introduce herself. My name is Sandy and Stella is my sister, she needs a good man in her life. You know, someone to help her get her groove back."

Stella elbowed Sandy in the side trying to keep her quiet.

"Well ladies this is my stop and I really have to get off." He turned to Stella, "If it's meant to be, our paths shall meet." He rang the bell signaling that he wanted to get off at the next stop.

Stella and Sandy watched Cal as his umbrella blend with the rain as the bus drove off.

Two week passed, Cal was in the Tampa Bay Mall and he saw this lady eye balling him. He was on the second floor and headed into the Champs Shoe store when he saw her coming up the steps. As he entered the store she approached him. She was wearing some white pants that looked like Picasso personally painted them onto her, with a gray blouse and gray heels to match. "Boy, you gotta be the finest man that I've seen in two weeks."

"Oh is that so? Is that a compliment or you're just comparing me to the last fine guy you saw?"

"You are the last fine guy I saw, memba, on the bus, I didn't have any money?"

"St..Stel.."

"Stella-Mae, yep that's me." She stated with her hand on her hip.

"Wow, you look astonishing! When I saw you down there grilling me I almost asked you if you had E.B.P."

LOVE NOT TO LOVE
A SHORT STORY BY DEXTER BROCKMAN SR.

"What the hell is E.B.P?"

"You a girl, you know that old saying back in day when the girls would always say E.B.P., it means Eye Ball Problem."

"Naw, I don't remember that saying."

"So what's been good with you? The last time I saw you, you and your girl was all drippy and wet and your arm was in a sling."

"Not as wet as I want to be!" She mumbled under her breath. "Why thank you, you look quiet charming yourself."

"What brings you to this mall? You look like a man who loves an adventure. This mall is dead!"

"Well I have a lot of things going on in my life so when I want to shop I come to this mall because I know it's never packed."

"Well when you got off the bus you told me that if our paths would meet, then it was meant to be. Here we are."

"You said it backwards, it was 'If it's meant to b...'" she placed her hand over his lip so she could get his attention.

She dug her hand in her purse pulled out a pen and a piece of paper. "What's your number? We need to hook up some time." She leaned against the rail scratching the pen on the paper making sure pen had ink.

He leaned back to peep game, he knew there had to be a reason that she was asking for his number so he tests her, "What's your number? Let me get in contact with YOU some time." To his surprise she supplied him with it.

He gave her his number and she said, "Well I'll call you later tonight." And that was his confirmation that he was expecting.

COINCIDENTALLY MISHAPPENED
THE ANTHOLOGY

LOVE NOT TO LOVE
A SHORT STORY BY DEXTER BROCKMAN SR.

The conversation didn't last much longer before they went their separate ways.

Later that night Stella called Cal around 9ish and they made plans to hook up. Cal was living in a hotel suite that had two rooms with his brother who really wasn't his brother, but when Cal moved to Tampa he took him under his wings and introduced him to the game. They were running a trap (a Drug House) so they were picky about the people they brought over, but Cal assumed Stella was cool. Stella asked was it o.k. if she brought her sister with her and Cal agreed.

As soon as the girls made it they were segregated. Sandy went into the room with Cal's brother.
Stella and Cal sat on the couch and Cal said, "I have a bag of trick drug, what you wanna do?"

"What the hell is trick drug?" Stella asked.

"Trick drug is cocaine." He stated as he pulled out a fresh bag and placed it on the table.

"Why do you call it trick drug?" Stella asked.

"You can take this drug anywhere, like to the strip club or a regular one. When you pull it out, you don't have to trick anyone because this will do it for you." He explained.

Moments later Stella tore into the bag headfirst. Stella's past consisted of abusing drugs and abusive men. No matter how hard she tried, when she got away from one the other would always creep in.

They started some heavy touching, then the birds flew next to the bees and room was filled with sex, sweat and drugs. Stella was making so much noise that her sister (who was in the back room) came out and asked, "Stella, girl what he in there doing to you?"

She replied, "I don't know but he need to keep doing it!"

LOVE NOT TO LOVE
A SHORT STORY BY DEXTER BROCKMAN SR.

After a decent night of sex Cal was ready to take her home. Being that he was running a Trap out of that room the longer it was closed the more money he was missing. For some strange reason Stella didn't want Cal to drop her off, she and her sister caught a cab.

Cal and Stella had several episodes, but they always took place in the Trap or at another hotel room and Cal often questioned Stella about going to her apartment.

One particular night the Trap was hot. Police had just kicked in two rooms in that hotel looking for drugs so Cal and his brother had to get away for a while.

Stella agreed to let them come over. When Cal and his brother made it to the house, Stella and her sister greeted them with a hug at the door. It was Stella's apartment, only a one-bedroom. Stella let her sister and Cal's brother take the room. As they closed the door to the bedroom Cal pulled out the trick drug and it was on again, heavy breathing and Elvis reaching!

Around 11pm Cal had just got finish rolling a joint when a car pulled up. They could see the lights shining through the living room window. Stella got up and ran to the room to get her sister.

Doom, Doom, Doom, Doom! "I know you in there with somebody I saw the car in the driveway." Is what the guy yelled as he continued pounding the door.

Cal reached under the pillow and he pulled out his 9mm inserted the clip pulled the hammer back and placed it under back under the pillow.

Sandy came running out of the backroom and went to the door, "She ain't here, it's just me and I got company. I'll tell her that you came by."

There was silence for a few seconds and then Doom, Doom, Doom. Down came the door.

LOVE NOT TO LOVE
A SHORT STORY BY DEXTER BROCKMAN SR.

Stella was standing next to the window crying. Cal reached under the pillow and placed the 9mm on his lap making it visible. The guy looked over at Cal. "What's up?" The intruder spoke to Cal. In the next instant the guy turned and hit Stella in the face. He was punching her like she was a dude. Cal pulled out his lighter lit his joint and he watched the show as the guy picked Stella up over his and dropped her on the coffee table. She was screaming to Cal asking him to help but he was so high from the cocaine and weed that he thought he was watching a good movie in high definition. After the beat down session, Cal and his brother left and got a room on the other side of town.

Once they got established in the room Cal's brother came to him and ask, "Cal, man why didn't you help that girl when that dude was beating her?"
Cal sat there reminiscing on the things that he'd seen in his past. He just shook his head in shame with no words.
"You know what Sandy told me?"
Cal looked up at his lil' brother standing over him with concern for what Sandy had poisoned into his brother's mind.
"Sandy told me that she and Stella knew you from a long time ago."
Cal dropped his head and placed his hands over his face, "I know lil' bro, that's why I let that hoe get beat down. All I can think about was how them hoes set my cousin up when we were young. That day on the bus when I met them I knew who they were, and I told her, 'If it was meant to be, our paths will meet.' They finally did."
Cal placed his hands together and rest his chin on his fist and said, "Love not to love lil' bro, Love not to love!"
That night when the police came to Stella's they arrested her for having cocaine all over the house. She spent a year in a rehab treatment.

LOVE NOT TO LOVE
A SHORT STORY BY DEXTER BROCKMAN SR.

Later that week Cal got busted with cocaine and he was sentenced to one year in the county jail. His lil' brother got him a lawyer that cut a deal with the state and Cal was released to an outpatient Drug Rehab.

Coincidentally it was the same Drug Rehab that Stella was finishing up her six months. He never said anything to her about the incident that happened in Palm Beach when he was a kid, nor did she ever say anything to him about the night he watched her get the super beat down.

Both of them cleaned up their acts, became the best of friends and they're living drug free. They have been together for about three years plus they have child on the way!

The reason I know so much about "he"? Well, because that "he" be ME!

Death is the Beginning
A Short Story by Jamie Bush

DBROCKMAN PUBLISHING PRESENTS:

DEATH IS THE BEGINNING

A SHORT STORY BY: JAMIE BUSH

Coincidentally Mishappened
The Anthology
Death is the Beginning
A Short Story by Jamie Bush

The morning of September 23, 2000 proved to be a normal morning. The birds chirped, the sun rose and the moon fell from the sky. It wasn't a typical morning for me, however, because I awoke with a strange feeling in my belly that something major was going to happen today. Being that it was Saturday I hurried to turn on the TV to watch ESPN's College Game Day show.

Midway thorough it the strange feeling in my gut began to grow stronger as if it was trying to tell me something. As I began to think about what it was that was bothering me I caught a glimpse of my graduation picture. It was a picture of my parents and me holding each other. The last time I had spoken with my mother was Thursday afternoon around two o'clock.

I called to leave a message but she unexpectedly answered the phone. She acted as if she was really happy to hear from me. She told me that she had been ill for about two weeks and was going to the doctor on Friday to get checked out. Naturally I was worried. I asked her would it be alright if I came home this weekend so I could be with her and brighten up her spirit, but she declined and said everything would be alright, and that I brighten her spirit everyday by growing to being the man that I am.

DEATH IS THE BEGINNING
A SHORT STORY BY JAMIE BUSH

My mother was always saying little things like that to ease my worries so I figured that everything would be alright. We expressed our love to each other and got off the phone. Little did I know that this was the last time I would ever hear my mother's comforting words again.

I had a Biology exam coming up on Monday so I got out my notes and began to study them when the same feeling in my gut grew even stronger. I could do nothing to get this feeling out of my mind. A few hours passed and I was completely engulfed in my biology notes when the strange feeling got the best of me. I went into a state of panic about my mother. I called home again to see how her doctor's visit went. I got the answering machine, but hearing her voice on it helped the situation a little. I was still worried, so I left a concerned message and hung up the phone.

A few minutes later I decided to call my older brother Chris and talk with him for a while to see if that would help. Chris has always been there for me like a big brother should, so his words were always comforting. He is a little eccentric but everything he does has good purpose behind it. As soon as he picked up the phone he could detect the presence of trouble in my voice. I told him

DEATH IS THE BEGINNING
A SHORT STORY BY JAMIE BUSH

that my mother was sick and she had been to the doctor to see what was wrong and I hadn't heard from her since then. I did it in sort of a frantic tone so he calmed me down and let me know everything was alright and that he would call the house and check on her himself. So again I was put at ease and the strange feeling in my gut went away.

I decided that I had done enough studying for that day and tuned into the Florida State-Louisville game that was on ESPN2. FSU was dominating as usual so I tuned my focus to getting out of the house. My room had begun to beat me down with all the worry that was in the air. I got out some clothes and jumped into a hot shower that seemed to last for an eternity. As the water trickled off of my brown-skinned physique I could feel the strange feeling drift away as if it was following the water down into the drain.

I got out and got dressed in a flash and bounced out of the house headed towards my comrade's place to enjoy a festive evening of marijuana and alcohol. I was half way down the steps when I realized that I forgot to put on a belt, so I bolted back into the apartment to properly equip myself with the right gear when the phone

DEATH IS THE BEGINNING
A SHORT STORY BY JAMIE BUSH

startled me. I looked at the caller ID and saw unavailable so I figured that it was someone from back home calling to check up on me. I answered in a cheerful manner and came to find out that it was my cousin Derrick on the phone. Derrick was a straight-forward type dude because of his military background. What he would tell me in the next few minutes would change my life forever. He told me to sit down and listen to him carefully.

"Jamie, your mother is in the hospital and it doesn't look good."

Those words ripped through me like a pack of wolves pouncing on some weak prey. I fell to my knees and the tears began to trickle down my face.

I screamed to him, "What the hell do you mean she's in the hospital and it doesn't look good? What the hell is she doing in the hospital?"

He told me that she went to hospital Friday morning to get some gallstones removed from her stomach and that her heart stopped once she was being prepped for surgery. I honored his honesty because in situations like that most people will tell you anything to keep your spirit up. After Derrick alerted me to what was about to go he handed the phone to my father. He told me that my

DEATH IS THE BEGINNING
A SHORT STORY BY JAMIE BUSH

mother had ordered him not to tell me because she didn't want me to worry. He repeated Derrick words but he did it with the comfort of a loving father. He told me that the whole family was at the hospital giving him all the support that he needed and that he was ok regarding his present circumstances.

He put Derrick back on the phone and he told me that I needed to get home as soon as possible. I told them that I could catch the Greyhound in the morning but he was like "Jaime, you need to get here tonight son. Your mother is dying and calling for you!"

I told him that I had my half of the apartment's electric bill, which was enough to get me home that night. He mentioned that I should fly because time was precious. So I called the Tallahassee Regional Airport to see if they had anything available going towards the Tampa/St. Petersburg area and they didn't. I called him back and told him the soonest I could get there was six in the morning. He accepted my plan and told me to come home expecting the worst. I called my friend Kirsten and briefed her with my present situation and ask if she could take me to the Greyhound Station as soon as possible. I turned to her because she had always been there for me and I

DEATH IS THE BEGINNING
A SHORT STORY BY JAMIE BUSH

love her like a sister. I packed a few things and headed out the door, but before I could get there I broke down and began to cry because I just couldn't picture my life without the person I loved the most in it. I called my friend Shakeena and let her know what was going on and she calmed me down and told me to put it in God's hands and not worry, for if it is God's will it shall be done. As I approached the bottom of my apartment steps Kirsten showed up. She was accompanied by another friend of mine named Cory. He was a strong young brother who always welcomed you as if you were a brother dear to his heart. His presence helped as I piled my things in Kirsten's champagne colored Chevy Malibu. I mentioned this because my mother drove the exact same car but the color was maroon.

Kirsten zoomed me to the bus station and asked me if I knew when I would be back. I greeted her with a blank stare and shook my head as if I answered her with words she already knew. The bus station was shockingly cold and empty for a Saturday night. I purchased my bus tickets and proceeded to wait on the bus. The time I arrived was around 11:15pm and the next bus to Clearwater was leaving at 12:40am, so I hopped on the

DEATH IS THE BEGINNING
A SHORT STORY BY JAMIE BUSH

phone and told my dad when to expect me home. His voice on the other end sounded like a man whose heart had been broken. His words told me without telling what I was about to find out.

12:40am came around pretty swiftly as I loaded myself and my belonging onto the bus. That six hour bus ride was the longest that I have ever lived through. It seemed like the hands of time tortured me with every passing millisecond. It was like my heart was being strangled and my mind was being beaten by the thoughts and memories that I would soon be clutching like a newborn to his mother's nipple. I found some comfort in a very bright star that shined high in the sky. As long as I could find that star I figured my mother was ok.

As I pulled into the Tampa bus station I hurried to call my dad to tell him where I was, but there was no answer at the hospital phone. I called my house to see if he was there but the answering machine picked up right away and it was my mother's voice. Hearing her voice hurt me like it never hurt before so I slammed the phone down. I called Derrick but there was no answer at his home either.

**DEATH IS THE BEGINNING
A SHORT STORY BY JAMIE BUSH**

I switched buses and headed for Clearwater, and as we pulled into the bus station I saw another familiar face. It was Coach Joseph Marshall, a man I saw as an Uncle who I could chat with from time to time. He was also a good friend of my mother and family. The look on his face told me what I was about to find out...my mother was gone.

I packed my things into the truck and we sped off towards my house. I tried to initiate some conversation but his words were minimal as if his mind was reaching for something but his arms were too short. We reached my house and it felt totally empty, as if no one lived there. It was an eerie felling. I dropped my things and told coach to take me to my Aunt's house. As we pulled up to her house that strange feeling in my gut began to reveal itself again but it came along with another feeling called "You're about to hear something you already knew."

My Aunt Glenn greeted me at the door with a tear soaked face and hugged me like she never hugged me before. Next was my uncle Israel who repeated her actions. My dad crawled out of the bed and approached me with a heavy heart. He grabbed me and hugged me tight, the kind of tightness as if he was trying to hold on to a piece

DEATH IS THE BEGINNING
A SHORT STORY BY JAMIE BUSH

of something that was already gone. Then he looked me square in the eyes and he rubbed my shoulders. The death soaked tears streamed down his face as his lips began to move…

"She's gone Jamie." He mumbled.

At that moment I had an "out of body" experience as I could see my father holding me. My body just went limp like a soggy, wet corn flake. The woman who gave me life, the woman who nourished me when I was sick, the woman whose tender touch could ease away any pain and suffering that engulfed me was gone…FOREVER!

I screamed, but no words came out. I cried but no tears would fall because deep inside I knew that in this type of process, death is only…THE-BEGINNING.

DBROCKMAN PUBLISHING PRESENTS:

ROOM 423

A SHORT STORY BY: BOB CAIN

ROOM 423
A SHORT STORY BY BOB CAIN

It was no wonder that to all who knew him, Leo Osgood lived alone. He had experienced enough during his four-year enlistment in the Army that he was content to not talk about it; and, although he was kind and a true gentleman, Leo was a loner, and to the folks around it appeared he had always lived in Room 423, four floors up in the corner.

There is something about fives. After his birth in London in 1925, his mother and father arrived in America and took up residency in Room 502. Yet, after a faulty electrical cable took the fifth floor in 1935, the family relocated to Room 423. Soon it was Mom, Dad and the five children, and for a brief while, everyone was happy most of the time. Then life happened and the world happened to be less than kind. In 1955, when Leo returned from the service, Mom passed away, and then Dad 10 years later, leaving him, as the oldest, in charge of the home. Both twin sisters moved out earlier in 1955, never married, and passed away in 1965 within five weeks of each other. They were only 35. One brother died in Germany in 1945, and the youngest brother committed suicide shortly after he heard his only son, Leo's nephew, was killed in Desert Storm.

ROOM 423
A SHORT STORY BY BOB CAIN

It is here the story unfolds. Leo is standing at the dining room window and listening to the birds sing as blue, yellow and red wings flash through the tops of the trees that run unobstructed from the downtown business district bordering Market Street to the edge of the hillside reservoir. In the distance the Sunday afternoon carillon program has just ended, and Leo's spirit is uplifted.

"Come and listen to the beautiful songs we will sing for you," the birds seem to say. It had been quite some time since Leo had actually felt this much at peace. "Come and we will sing . . . "

KNOCK   KNOCK   KNOCK

He quietly shuffled to the door and looked through the peephole.   In his haste, unfortunately Leo had forgotten to remove the reading glasses that were on his forehead and they tapped against the door.

Leo froze with fear. *(Shit) he thought (maybe she didn't hear them)*

"Leo? Leo, are you THERE?" *(Oh no, please dear god not now. Not Thelma. I know . . . I'll just be quiet and she'll go away. That's it. I'll just be extremely very quiet and maybe she'll go . . .)*

KNOCK   KNOCK   KNOCK

ROOM 423
A SHORT STORY BY BOB CAIN

(Aghhhhh, the witch has ears like a bat) he thought. *(shit shit shit.)*

"Open up, Mr. Osgood. It's me . . . Thelma. I know you're in there. Just open the door Mr. Osgood. I have something I need to tell you and it won't take too much of your time." *(Oh god, oh NO WAY.)*

"Go away, Thelma. I'm busy," he lied. He didn't like lying to her and especially on Sunday, but *'damn it'* it was his Sunday, and he wanted to go and stand by the dining room window. He wanted to eat arsenic-laden glass shards and gargle with gasoline. He wanted to cut his toenails and defrost the fridge. Oh, it was still early and there was still time to iron everything in the closet and clean the kitty litter in the kitchen. "Go AWAY," he said as he grabbed the Oreck.

The deafening noise of the vacuum filled Thelma with unbridled joy. Since Old Grumpy was in and he was listening, why not give him something special to listen to she thought.

KNOCK KNOCK KNOCK KNOCK KNOCK KNOCK KNOCK-KNOCK-KNOCK KNOCK KNOCK KNOCK KNOCK KNOCK KNOCK KNOCK-KNOCK-KNOCK KNOCK KNOCKETY-KNOCKKNOCK KNOCKKNOCK

ROOM 423
A SHORT STORY BY BOB CAIN

. . . She pounded on the door, like a woman possessed, and when the noise stopped, so did the vacuum.

Leo yelled through the door, "Okay, O - KAY, you have my attention. What the HELL do you WANT?"

Thelma paused for effect, got closer to the door and took a deep breath. She was winning. Quietly and with great joy, matter-of-factly, like a mother speaking to an extremely naughty, spoiled five-year-old, Thelma spoke. "I want you to let me in."

With unimaginable reservation, Leo unlocked the door. "This better not take long." he said. "I'm busy."

"Thanks for letting me in, Mr. Osgood," she sang as she, shrouded in her grotesque storybook-knit sweater, flitted across a clean living room carpet and flopped down hard upon his dead mother's antique brocade sofa like a rare leviathan gooney bird from hell. Here now – overpowering as a breeze of Yardley Lilac, in white Capri chukka pants and gold sandals – perched the creature that had on many occasions visited him late at night only to devour his entire stock of pecan sandies as it screeched about everything in just the whole world.

(god give me strength) he prayed.

ROOM 423
A SHORT STORY BY BOB CAIN

"Well, what is it? What do you want, Thelma? There are no cookies, but would you like some tea and some toast and jam?"

"No. No thanks," she said.

Thelma was once a butterfly, but now only the moth remained. Yet under her 78 year-old exterior laid the soul of a spiked watermelon. To all appearances ... she was just a plain, old watermelon *with a plug taken out of it*, and *this* is what Thelma brought to the picnic. *Go on, have a slice. It's summer. It's Thelma!*

"Well what seems to be the issue, Thelma ... dear?" Leo asked as he sat in his favorite chair beside the sofa. He could be very nice to her under these circumstances.

She had always called him when she was off to the market for groceries, asking him if there was anything he needed or wanted. She took care of him and brought him his medicine after his slip-and-fall left him trapped in bed and under her watchful eye and talons for almost six months last year. And everyday, like clockwork, Thelma would call him on the phone *(to see if he had died during the night)*, and she would use the excuse of the call to bring him her used daily newspaper and letters from her family to read. So, under these circumstances, he thought

**ROOM 423
A SHORT STORY BY BOB CAIN**

he should throw caution to the wind and be a little civil to the "thorn in his side" that was Thelma.

Thelma cleared her throat and Leo never remembered her ever looking so serious as she did now.

"Well, it seems like I'm invited to move to Tampa to visit with my grandson and his family. They have a new baby, my great-grandson, William. You know the one that was born last November. Well, they said they sure could use an extra hand around the house down there . . . and what with baby-sitters being so dear . . ."

(Was she waiting for him to applaud?)

Leo arose and walked toward the window as he spoke. "Well, what did you tell them you would do? You said you would go, didn't you?"

"Well, sure I did," she said. "You and everyone else here know just how crazy I am about warm weather, and they have everything for me down there – sunshine, orange juice, amusement parks and now the new baby. I put in my notice and I should be gone by the middle of July. If there is anything you need or you'd like to have from my place, let me know, otherwise it's just going to the Good Will.?"

ROOM 423
A SHORT STORY BY BOB CAIN

Suddenly Leo realized that soon she would be gone. Outside the bright colors of the birds turned to gray in his watering eyes, and a small tear fell on his cheek. It was like the time when his twin sisters whom he loved so very much decided to move on (and he never saw them alive again after they left.) Now Thelma was planning to leave, and there was nothing he could do about it. Nothing at all.

"Leo? Leo?"

"Yes."

"I should go, shouldn't I?" she asked.

"Of course you should. Sure, I'll help you with whatever you need, just say the word. Florida will be great for you and just think about all the fun you'll h-have." His voice cracked as he turned to look into the eyes of the woman he had always loved. He never noticed before that her eyes had violet rings around the blue irises, or how remarkable they looked in the golden light of the Sunday afternoon sun.

He remembered so many things: Wasn't this the same woman who had always brought him the paper and left the crossword puzzles for him to do? Didn't she also bake some of the best chocolate chip cookies in the world

ROOM 423
A SHORT STORY BY BOB CAIN

and share them with him every time she made a batch? Didn't she keep the neighbors quiet when he needed to sleep, and crawl through the apartment picking up his laundry and bringing it back all clean and ironed when he couldn't do it for himself?

Yes, there was no doubt at all he loved her, and his heart was breaking. What right did he have to stand in the way of her happiness? None.

"Well, it's settled then," she said as she rose from the couch and walked over to be beside him at the window. "I can't go," she said, coming closer to him than she had ever been before.

She took him by the hand.

"Don't you see, Leo. Sure, I could go to Florida and I could have all those things and everything I ever wanted. But I wouldn't have you to take care of, and I wouldn't always be able to ask you if you were alright. Without you would always be a horrible mistake. And after I was there for a month or two, I know I remember you and now, and I would always wonder if I had left 1-love, real love, just pass me by."

Leo lifted his hand to wipe away the tear that had fallen on her cheek.

ROOM 423
A Short Story by Bob Cain

"But my apartment . . .? "

"Don't worry, Thelma," he said, pulling her closer to him than he had ever dared to before.

"But the baby . . . ?"

"Please, don't worry," he said as kissed her and whispered that he loved her. "They'll come up for the wedding."

"Really?"

"Really."

"I was in hell, Leo. You know I could have never gone on with the move. You see, I have always loved you."

"Stay with me then," he said, as he kissed her again. "Stay and listen to the birds with me."

DBROCKMAN PUBLISHING PRESENTS:

TYPICAL SUNDAY AFTERNOON

A SHORT STORY BY: DBROCKMAN SR.

Coincidentally Mishappened
The Anthology
Typical Sunday Afternoon
A Short Story by D. Brockman Sr

One Sunday afternoon after an intense message from Dr. Price I put together a college throwback grilled egg and cheese toast. Then I chose to settle into my couch and prepare myself for a new week the traditional male way, Sunday football. While watching my All-Time favorite quarterback Dan Marino on the Pre-Game show it took about two swigs from my tall glass of Kool-Aid before I got "the 'itis'". My eyes started feeling like they were carrying anvils.

The food settles and it was over, lights out. I was out for about thirty minutes, and when I woke up the Dolphin's game was already in progress. Through my peripheral I saw a shadow, but I paid it no attention until I heard a noise in my kitchen. My first instinct told me to go see what was going on in there. I thought to myself maybe I forgot to turn the stove off and a dishrag caught on fire. But, being the analytical person I am, if there was a fire I would have smelled smoke. My second instinct asked questions such as; did I forget to lock the door and someone entered while I was asleep? I turned towards my kitchen and I saw the shadow again. My heart muscles starting overacting, I could feel the blood rushing through my veins. I made an attempt to gather my thoughts and figure out how I was going to approach this issue. I removed myself from the couch but I could barely move. I suddenly felt like I was a thousand pounds and I could barely keep my eyes open. Then I heard a noise again, and it sound as if it was directly behind me. I turned around as swiftly as I could to face whatever was behind me. Nothing...there was absolutely nothing behind me.

I started to walk towards the kitchen and visualized the shadow again. I returned to my sectional, but a trip normally would take about four good steps from one side of my couch to the other seemed to last an eternity. I closed my eyes and ran for two seconds only to open them and find that I was stationary, still in the SAME spot! I looked at my television and the Dolphins had just thrown an interception for a touchdown. I couldn't focus on that though, I had greater problems ahead. I retrieved a bat from the corner beside my computer. My adrenaline rose, anticipating that something was about go down right here in the privacy of my own home. I'm sweating, my eyes are still heavy and I still feel like I weigh a thousand pounds. Don't feel this will be one of my best battles, but a man ain't a man if he doesn't protect his home.

Coincidentally Mishappened
The Anthology
Typical Sunday Afternoon
A Short Story by D. Brockman Sr

Suddenly I heard keys rattling at the door. I thought to myself again...who as access to my apartment? Could it be my Angel? Naw, a key wasn't provided to her. Maybe it was my older brother? Naw, that was at my last apartment. No one I know has a key to my apartment. Still I continue to here someone entering a key into my lock. I made a drastic move to hide behind my sectional to get an edge on whoever was coming through my door. Then I heard my cousin open my door and it sounded as if he was on his cell phone. I leapt from behind the sofa, and while stretching myself out I realized I didn't have on any clothing below my waist. My cousin replied "I'm sorry Cuz, I didn't know you were naked!" Then I woke up.

DBROCKMAN PUBLISHING PRESENTS:

DAD'S ADVICE

A SHORT STORY BY: TAMMEAKA GRAHAM

DAD'S ADVICE
A SHORT STORY BY TAMMEAKA GRAHAM

Blinking hard, Lacey tried to focus in the dark room. Her wrists burned from where the ropes were cutting into her flesh. The pain in her left leg was excruciating. Her ankle was broken. She was sure of that. What she wasn't sure of was how she ended up in this situation. She thought she knew it all; that she had everything all figured out. If only she had listened to her father. She should have just let him drop her off at Donna's house, but she had to be stubborn and now look at where it has gotten her. Lacey moved slowly around in the dark, scooting across what felt like a cement floor, wincing in pain as she accidentally put too much weight on her ankle. Damn it, she thought. I can't see anything. Slowly, she composed herself and began to concentrate on the rope restraining her wrist. She flexed the muscles in her wrists and forearms and felt the rope start to slacken. Sweat poured off of her face as she worked the rope. Finally, after 10 minutes, she felt the rope slacken enough to where she could wriggle free. "Yes," Lacey cried out in relief. Her eyes had adjusted to the dark and she was able to make out shapes in the room. Slowly, she raised her self up, putting all of her weight on her right leg. She began to work her way along the wall when suddenly the lights in the room came on. Lacey was blinded by the sudden brightness. As her eyes began to adjust to the light, she looked around the room. She was in what appeared to be a cellar of some kind. There were empty wine racks covered in dust. The floor was concrete and also covered in a layer of dust. She clearly could see where she had been dragged into the room. Boxes were stacked against the back wall. As she scanned the room, her heart nearly stopped when she noticed a pool of blood on the floor. As Lacey's eyes, wide with fear, followed the path of the blood she saw its source. There was a figure on the floor, balled

Dad's Advice
A Short Story by Tammeaka Graham

in the fetal position. Lacey hobbled over to the figure and knelt by it.

"Hello?" She called out questioningly. "Ummm, are you ok?" The figure remained in its position. Hesitantly, she reached out to it. The body rolled onto its back and looked up at Lacey with dead eyes. Lacey's terrified screams echoed throughout the room.

Jason Fitzpatrick had been up all night long. His 17-year-old daughter Lacey was missing. She had left last night around 6:30pm for a study party at her friend Donna's house. When Lacey had not returned by 10:00pm he began to worry. He called and was informed by a sleepy Donna that Lacey had not made it to the party. Jason knew instantly something was wrong. After frantically calling Lacey's cell phone and only getting her voicemail, Jason called the police. Officers arrived at the home and took Jason's statement. They advised him that his daughter probably lied about going to her friend's house and met up with her boyfriend. Jason filed the report anyway. They didn't know Lacey the way he did. He knew his daughter would not lie about something like that. They had their battles but she had never lied to him. Not even when it came to that punk Rick.

Rick Templeton came into Lacey's life a couple of months ago. He had recently just come back to town after being gone for six years. Something about a medical condition he had that required treatment in an obscure a facility in upstate New York. His father, Mark Templeton, was one of the town's few wealthy residents. He called Angels Grove home but the man was hardly ever around. His newest endeavor was in Africa where he had been for the last six months.

DAD'S ADVICE
A SHORT STORY BY TAMMEAKA GRAHAM

Rick was definitely the type of kid who was got what he wanted, and at any cost. Jason did not like him at all. Rick lacked respect for any kind of authority and that disrespect ultimately carried over to the authority that Jason had over Lacey.   After many battles with Lacey over Rick, Jason had enough. He remembered the last time Lacey had seen Rick. "Nice of you to come home, "Jason said flatly to Lacey as she strolled into the house at 11:00pm on a Thursday night.

"Sorry I'm late dad," Lacey said in a shaky voice.

" Sorry you're late..." was Jason's reply. Lacey kept her head down and did not reply. Her hair was disheveled and covered her face.

"Were you out with Rick again?" Jason asked. Lacey turned her head toward the door.

"Yes," she mumbled. Jason heard something wrong in her voice.

"Lacey?" He called out to her. "What's wrong?"

"Nothing Daddy, I'm just tired," she said unconvincingly.

"Lacey, look at me," he commanded. Lacey turned her back to him and began to uncontrollable sob. Jason grabbed her by her shoulders and spun her around. What he saw invoked the worst kind of rage. He fought the emotion and looked softly into his daughters eyes. Her beautiful green eyes were marred with tears. The right eye was red and swollen, sure to be black and blue in the morning. Her shirt was ripped and there was something that looked like blood underneath her fingernails.

"Lacey?" Jason asked softly. "What happened, honey?"

"Oh, Daddy," sobbed Lacey. "Rick...," she mumbled into his shoulder as he hugged her.

Dad's Advice
A Short Story by Tammeaka Graham

"Lacey, I need to know what happened. Look at me, honey. Tell me what he did". Jason walked Lacey to the couch and sat her down. A tearful Lacey explained how she and Rick had driven to the park and were sitting in his car when Rick began to pressure her into having sex with him. Lacey told him she was not ready for that. Jason shuddered as he thought of what the implications of that statement were. Lacey continued, telling her father how Rick called her a daddy's girl and that she would never be a real woman until she gave it up. When Lacey still refused Rick slapped her across her face and ripped her blouse. Lacey scratched him in the eyes and stumbled out of the car and ran off as he shrieked in pain. Rick screamed for her to come back. "Dad, why'd he do that to me?" she asked, as she looked up and into her father's eyes. "I thought he really cared about me." Jason felt his stomach knot. This is not the way he wanted his daughter to learn about the world; that people like Rick were not as few and far in between as people pretend to believe. That bastard, he thought to himself. If he ever got his hands on him...

"Lacey, I'm calling the police and filing a report," Jason said.

"NO! Daddy, please no!" Lacey begged her father.

" Lacey, he hurt you. Can't you understand that? He needs to be put behind bars so he can never hurt anyone else again," Jason replied.

"No daddy, I can't go through that. I won't see him anymore. I just want to forget it every happened," Lacey sobbed hysterically. "Please daddy, for me, please just leave it alone. I can't.." she broke down and cried into his chest. Jason felt his heart breaking. He wanted so badly to teach that punk kid a lesson, but he did not want Lacey to be hurt anymore. Reluctantly, he obliged his daughter

Dad's Advice
A Short Story by Tammeaka Graham

as long as she promised that if Rick ever approached her again, she would press charges. Now, as he sat alone at the kitchen table trying not the think the worst, he regretted not pushing the issue. He was sure that Templeton kid had something to do with Lacey's disappearance. He got up and grabbed his jacket as he walked out the front door. He was going to find answers and he knew exactly where to start.

Mark Templeton had just finished his morning coffee when he heard the doorbell ring. He ignored it. After all, that's what he was paid Maria for. He was taking a bite out of his bagel when he heard raised voices coming from the foyer. "I don't give a damn if he walked from Africa on snowshoes! Get him out here," Mark heard a male voice yell.

"It's ok, Maria," Mark said, coming into the foyer. "Please show Mr... Sir, what is your name?"

"Jason. Jason Fitzpatrick"

"Maria, please show Mr. Fitzpatrick into my study. Coffee, Mr. Fitzpatrick?" Mark asked.

"No thank you" Jason replied.

Jason followed Maria into the study. She ushered him into a chair and quickly left the room, closing the doors behind her. Mark took a cigar from a humidor on his desk. He offered one to Jason.

"No thank you" Jason replied. "I am not here to indulge in pleasantries, Mr. Templeton." Jason said rather sternly.

"Yes, I could tell from the shouting in the foyer that something has upset you. How can I be of help to you, Mr. Fitzgerald?" Mark asked.

"My daughter Lacey is missing. She didn't make it home last night." Jason answered.

DAD'S ADVICE
A SHORT STORY BY TAMMEAKA GRAHAM

"I am sorry to hear that, Mr. Fitzpatrick. I can understand why that would upset you. Is there some way that I can be of service to you?" Mark asked concerned.

"Yes, actually you can. Where might I find your son?" Jason asked.

"My son?" asked Mark surprised. "Did you say you were looking for my son?"

"Yes, your son Rick," Jason replied.

"Mr. Fitzpatrick, I don't know why you would be looking for Rick. I am absolutely certain that your daughter is not with my son." Mark replied.
"Really?" Jason said insidiously. "What makes you so sure of that?"

"Because Mr. Fitzpatrick, Rick died six years ago," Mark answered.

"What?" Jason asked dumbstruck.

"Yes. Rick died six years ago from complications of an appendectomy. He was 14-years-old."

"That is impossible. I saw him for myself. He's been in my house." Mark said.

"Mr. Fitzpatrick, I don't doubt that there was a young man at your home but there is no possible way it could be my Rick. When doctors discovered that Rick had a potentially fatal, rare blood disease, my ex-wife and I took Rick to the Children's Hospital in upstate New York where he could be treated and possibly cured. While there he suffered an appendicitis and died on the operating table. His mother couldn't bear the thought of bringing him home for a funeral so we had a discreet ceremony at the hospital. Rick is buried in the hospital cemetery." Mark explained to Jason. Jason was speechless.

"I am not sure who this young man is, but I can assure you that my son Rick is not with your daughter. I am sorry that I cannot be of more help to you. Now, if you

Dad's Advice
A Short Story by Tammeaka Graham

would please excuse me, I need to get to the office. I have a meeting with the board of directors. Maria will see you out."

Jason, still in shock, walked down the driveway to his car. Dead? Rick Templeton was dead and had been dead for six years. Who the hell had been in his house with his daughter? As he got into his car he felt a terrible sinking feeling in his stomach. He did not know where to go from here. Not knowing where to go from this point, Jason had a terrible sinking feeling in his stomach. He had to find Lacey, he thought. He had to find her fast.

Lacey sat against the wall. The body in the room with her was that of a girl that seemed to be around Lacey's age. She didn't recognize the girl, but she probably looked different when she was alive—with the rest of her face intact. Lacey fought the urge to vomit. "Think, Lacey. Think," she whispered to herself. Slowly, she rose to her feet, using the wall as a brace. Her ankle throbbed with pain, but she was able to put a small amount of weight on it. She scanned the room looking for a way out. She made her way around the boxes and spotted a small window up near the ceiling. There was no way she was getting up there. Even if she could somehow get up there with a broken ankle, there was no way she could fit through that window. All of a sudden she heard heavy footsteps directly above her. With each step dust was loosened from the ceiling beams. They were coming toward the door. Lacey hobbled as quickly as she could back to where she had awakened. She lied down with her hands behind her back and eyes closed. Just as the footsteps reached the door she remembered the ropes. She quickly slipped her hands into them and laid face down with her eyes closed. She heard the door open. The stairs creaked with every step that was taken. She could

Dad's Advice
A Short Story by Tammeaka Graham

feel her assailant hovering above her and pretended to still
be unconscious. She felt breath on her face while strange
fingers pushed strands of hair away from her face. Lacey
fought the urge to open her eyes and see her attacker's
face. "Sleep Lacey. Rest up," a man's voice said. "You
will need energy for what I have in store for you," the voice
said with a laugh. Lacey remained still as she heard him
shuffling around the room. She kept up her closed until
she heard the door close and the slowly fade away.
Slowly, she sat up and let ropes fall from her hands. She
immediately noticed that the girl's body was gone. That's
what he had come for. The scent of his cologne lingered in
the air. Joop. Lacy knew it well. She didn't have to see
here attacker's face. Lacey knew who he was. She had
once bought a bottle for her ex-boyfriend. She knew that
cologne, but more importantly, she knew that voice. It
was Rick.
Jason was running out of time. He knew he had to find
Lacey, but he was out of leads. Then he remembered
something. He had seen Rick, if that was even his name,
with another boy. What was his name? Marcus! That
was it. Marcus Winston. Jason knew Marcus's father
David. David owned the sawmill where he was currently
the floor supervisor. Marcus would have to know
something. Jason drove to the Lemmie's on 5th Avenue.
Lemmie's was the town pool hall and local teen hangout
because anyone sixteen and older was allowed in. Marcus
was the town pool champion and Lemmie's was his second
home. Jason sped down the street and turned into the
parking lot. It was just as he expected. There was Marcus'
red Expedition in the parking lot. Hmmm, Jason thought
to himself. It must be nice to have a rich dad.
      The atmosphere in Lemmie's is that of any other
pool hall. Clouds of cigarette smoke lingered in the air

DAD'S ADVICE
A SHORT STORY BY TAMMEAKA GRAHAM

while deep fryers mingled with the scent of cheap perfume. This was teen heaven for a small town. Jason headed to the bar and sat on one of the bar stools. Eddie, the bartender, was busy getting beers to a group of girls. Jason waited till he rang up the tab before calling out to him.

"Eddie!" Jason yelled above the music. Eddie turned in his direction and gave him a big smile.

"Hey, Jay!" Eddie yelled back as he made his way over to Jason. "How ya doing? Ain't seen you here in a while?"

"Wish I could say things were going well but they sure the hell aren't. Lacey's missing," Jason replied. Eddie's expression turned somber
"Damn, Jay. Sorry to hear that. Lacey never seemed like the type to run off. Wonder what caused that?" Eddie asked.

"Not what, who?" Jason said, his eyes burning with renewed anger. "Eddie what table is Marcus at today?" Jason asked.

"Marcus? He's at table nine in the back. He likes to be in the back cause he thinks I can't see them other guys buying him beer. I know about it but his daddy owns this place and I ain't making no trouble for myself." Eddie said" Yeah I hear ya." Jason said with full understanding. David Winston was not someone you wanted to mess with especially when it came to his son, but today Jason was just going to have to gamble with that cause Lacey meant more to him than his job or his life. Jason began to make his way to the back of the pool hall to table nine. He spotted Marcus in a Pittsburgh Steelers jersey, leaning against a wall, calmly smoking a cigarette. His eyes were half open and red. He was clearly high. Jason walked up to him.

DAD'S ADVICE
A SHORT STORY BY TAMMEAKA GRAHAM

"Marcus, I Need to talk to ya for a minute," Jason said. Marcus looked Jason up and down and smiled a sly, cocky smile.

"So talk, old man," Marcus snidely replied. Jason swallowed the anger building up in his throat. This little punk really did not want to get on his bad side. "I'm looking for Lacey. I think she might have met up with your friend Rick. Do you know where they might be?" Jason asked. Marcus played it cool, but for just a moment Jason could see an uneasy look pass across his face.

"Sorry dude. Ain't seen your daughter and I don't know anybody named Rick but thanks for dropping by," Marcus said, clearly dismissing Jason. Jason couldn't take his smug attitude anymore. He didn't have time to play games with this kid, not when Lacey could be in bad trouble. Jason turned as if to walk away from Marcus but suddenly grabbed one of the pool sticks from the rack and swung around, backing Marcus up against the wall. He held the pool stick sideways, pressing it into Marcus throat, choking him. "Now listen to me," Jason growled into Marcus's ear. "I don't have time to play your little games. I swear on my life I will kill you if you don't tell me what I need to know, so I am going to ask you one last time before I snap your windpipe like a pencil. Okay?" Marcus struggled. "Where is Rick and Lacey?" Marcus's tried to break free of Jason's grip, but Jason was stronger than any foreman's punk kid. Jason pushed the pool stick harder into Marcus' throat. Marcus began to turn blue and he shook his head violently. Jason took this as a sign that Marcus was willing to talk. Jason eased pressure off of the pool stick. Marcus' face flooded with color as he gasped for breaths of air. "Talk God damnit," Jason commanded.

DAD'S ADVICE
A SHORT STORY BY TAMMEAKA GRAHAM

"All right, dude. All right" Marcus said in between coughs. "His name ain't Rick. It's Taylor. Taylor Preston. I stopped hanging with the guy after I found out he lied about who he was and shit started disappearing from my house. I figured Lacey had found out too and that is why she had broken up with him. I don't know, man. The guy was crazy.   He said he had to have Lacey, like she was the final piece in some kind of demented puzzle. I just let him know to leave me alone and most people around here know when Marcus' says get, you get. I guess you didn't get that memo" Marcus replied, his cockiness starting to return. "My dad is going to have your ass, man," he added with a grin. Jason smiled back as he swept the pool stick under Marcus' right leg, knocking him on his rear end. Jason kneeled down beside him, pool stick back at Marcus' throat. "Yeah, he is, is he? Well, I don't think you're going to say anything to dear old dad about this conversation, are you?" Jason asked as he let one hand down from the pool stick and grabbed the baggie he had seen peeking out of Marcus's jacket when he first walked up to him.

"Looks to me like this is just enough green in here for a felony. Bet your prints are all over this bag.   Even daddy can't make that go away," Jason said removing the pool stick from Marcus's throat. Marcus paled.   He slowly rose to his feet and took a deep breath before giving in. "Aight man. Damn, you can't tell my pops about this. I can't go to jail, man. Listen, promise me you won't say nothing to my dad and I won't say nothing to my dad. We can call it even," Marcus said in a low humble tone. He knew Jason had him. There was no point in him pissing Jason off. He couldn't risk Jason going to the cops. His dad would disown him if he got arrested and he could forget his trust fund because one of the conditions was

DAD'S ADVICE
A SHORT STORY BY TAMMEAKA GRAHAM

that he had to keep a felony free criminal record. He looked nervously at Jason.   Jason smirked. He wasn't really going to say anything to Marcus's dad. He just needed a little leverage over the little punk till he got what he needed.   "Are you sure, Rick—I mean Taylor didn't say anything else about Lacey?" Jason asked. Marcus shook his head no. "Fine, then. We're even, for now," Jason said as he stuffed the bag in his pocket. He was halfway to his car when he heard Marcus yelling after him. "Hey," Marcus yelled. Jason stopped and waited for Marcus to catch up to him. "Hey man." Marcus said, trying to catch his breath. "I don't know if this means anything to you, but Taylor did talk about some chick named Linda. Said he would always chill with her on the lake. Don't know if that helps any. Anyway, thanks again for being cool about the green and all." Marcus said as he walked away. Jason didn't respond. It finally all made sense to him. Linda? He ran to his car and jumped in. Barely closing the door, he floored the gas pedal and peeled out of Lemmie's parking lot and turned left, heading toward the interstate. He knew exactly where Lacey was.

Lacey was stunned by her revelation. Why would Rick do this to her? What did he want? Lacey slowly rose to her feet. She was careful to keep the majority of her weight on her left leg. She had to find a way out. She didn't know what Rick wanted but she now knew that he was capable of murder and she did not intend to be his next victim. She surveyed the room. There were shelves on the wall to her right. She made her way slowly over to them and examined their contents. One shelf was full .of jars and small lids, like the one's used to make jelly preserves. The next shelf held some dusty papers and a broken picture frame. She was about to examine the next

DAD'S ADVICE
A SHORT STORY BY TAMMEAKA GRAHAM

shelf when something caught her eye. A piece of a photograph was sticking out of the stack of papers. Lacey didn't know why but it caught her attention. She quietly moved the papers that were atop it and dusted it off. The photograph was yellowed with age and water damaged but the faces in the picture were still clear. The picture was of a family, a young woman, maybe 19 or 20-years-old who sat with a little boy on her lap. A man stood behind them. They were smiling. The boy looked to be around 5 or 6-years-old but it was the woman in the picture that made Lacey's heart jump. The woman was her mother Linda. Lacey could not fathom whom those other people were in the picture or why her mother would be posing with them as if they were a happy family. She was deep in thought when she heard a thud over head. Lacey stopped and looked up at the ceiling. She heard footsteps and then a door slam. A few minutes later she heard a car start. He was leaving. This was her chance. Lacey waited patiently counting the minutes until she was sure he was gone. She carefully made her way to the stairs. She slowly climbed the stairs, her ankle burning with agonizing pain. As she made it to the door she realized that she was probably locked in and she didn't have a way to unlock the door. Frantically, she searched her pockets hoping to find something to help her. She found her ATM card in her back pocket. Funny, her dad always yelled at her about that. Every time he did her laundry he'd find her it in the washing machine. She took the card and carefully slid it between the lock and the doorframe. She was praying as she wiggled the card up and down and turned the knob. If this was a deadbolt she was out of luck. She continued to wiggle the card. Remarkably, she heard the click of the lock pushing back into the doorframe. She turned the knob and the door swung open. Lacey took a

Dad's Advice
A Short Story by Tammeaka Graham

deep breath and slowly inched herself into the hallway. She eased herself down the hallway, bracing herself against the wall. At the end of the hallway Lacey turned and found herself in a huge living room. The furniture was covered with sheets and the sheets were cover with dust. The color drained from her face as she realized all too well where she was. Lacey was at the Manor. She had not seen or been there in three years; not since the night she helped her father pull her mother's lifeless body from the lake.

Jason was glad that traffic on the pike was light. It was a good hour drive up to the Manor. He knew Lacey was there. What he didn't know was if she was still alive. As Jason raced down the road his thoughts drifted to that night three years ago when his whole world changed. He and Linda had wanted to take Lacey to the Manor for a little vacation away from the world. Lacey had never been to the Manor, they had only recently managed to come up with the money to complete all the renovations and repairs that needed to be done to make the manor safe again. Linda had not been there for at least six years. Jason had overseen all the repairs. It had been a birthday present for Linda.   They planned to stay for two weeks since Lacey was out of school for the summer. The days flew by. Jason had loved watching his wife and daughter in the kitchen baking batches of cookies and throwing flour at each other like little kids. He remembered the way Linda's eyes shined in the moonlight as they had made love on the balcony under the stars.   They took nature walks and explored the area and swam in the lake. The lake... Jason's eyes filled with tears as he thought about the last time he held Linda in his arms. She was cold and her green eyes were empty as he held her and cried out her name. Jason didn't know why she went out to the lake.

DAD'S ADVICE
A SHORT STORY BY TAMMEAKA GRAHAM

She complained of a slight headache after dinner and said she wanted to lie down. Jason had brought her a nighttime pain reliever and some water and lied with her until she dozed off. He and Lacey were in the living room playing a game of scrabble when they heard Bosco, the neighbor's, dog barking frantically. Jason told Lacey to stay where she was while he went outside to check on things. The family had agreed to keep an eye on the dog while the Yardley's went to visit a sick relative. All Jason needed was for something to happen to Bosco. He would never hear the end of it. Jason headed outside and followed the sound of the dog's barking. He was almost to the lake that the Manor overlooked. How in the hell did Bosco make it all the way over here? Jason thought to himself. "Bosco," Jason yelled. He whistled but the dog just kept relentlessly barking. Jason followed the barks when he finally caught sight of Bosco. The dog was at the edge of the dock pawing at the ground. Jason ran up to Bosco and turned to follow the dogs gaze. Linda was in the water weakly trying to keep herself a float. She was pale. Jason dove in the water just as Linda went under. He swam as hard and fast as he could but when he got to her it was too late. She had been in under far too long. Jason swam back to the water's edge carrying Linda's limp body behind him. Lacey was there waiting for him with tears streaming down her face. She helped him pull her mother out of the water. He sent Lacey to call for help while he gave Linda mouth to mouth. For a brief moment she opened her eyes and took a breath. She seemed to be trying to say something. Jason put his ear to her lips. Linda's last words were weak but clear as crystal. I didn't know," she whispered. Then, before he could tell her that he loved her, she closed her eyes and died. Jason didn't know how long he sat there cradling her in his arms as he

DAD'S ADVICE
A SHORT STORY BY TAMMEAKA GRAHAM

rocked back and forth. He didn't remember the ambulance coming or the doctor at the hospital telling him what he had already know—that Linda was not coming back. He could only remember her green eyes closing and knowing they would never open again. The next morning the circumstances of Linda's death had come to light. Apparently the pain reliever that Jason had given her was labeled incorrectly. He had, through no fault of his own, given Linda three times the normal dosage. The police speculated that Linda had taken a walk down to the lake before the medication had a chance to truly make its way into her system and that she simply had fallen off the dock into the water. The amount of medication in her body had made it impossible for Linda to swim back to shore. Jason didn't buy the story. There were too many inconsistencies, which he pointed out to the police. First, the medication that Linda took was a prescription she always had with her since she was prone to migraines. She had taken two on the way up to the Manor and suffered no ill effects, so how could the same medication now be at too strong of a dosage? Secondly he had laid there with Linda until she had fallen asleep. She had asked him to hold her until she dozed off.   If he had given her three times the normal dose then there would have been no way for her to have made it to the dock without any assistance, and if she had simply fallen off the dock then how did she end up in the middle of the lake?   Then there was Bosco. Bosco had been put up in his kennel that night. Jason had set it up in the garage of the Manor. How did he get out of the kennel and out of the garage with all the doors closed and locked? The police took the information down but Jason's complaints were futile. The house was secure with no sign of forced entry, not even a foot print outside that could be linked to anyone other

Dad's Advice
A Short Story by Tammeaka Graham

than the family and there was no sign of trauma to Linda's body. All Jason had was circumstantial evidence and without any hard evidence there was nothing the police could do about it.   Now, three years later, Jason was once again trying to save the life of the person that meant the most to him.

"Lacey," Jason said to himself. "I'm coming, baby. Please hold on."

Lacey didn't know why Rick brought her here or how he even knew about the manor. She had never spoken with him about it. Lacey was overwhelmed by emotion. She was terrified, hurt, and full of questions. Slowly Lacey crept through the living room toward the window. She carefully pulled back the curtains and peeked outside. The sun was just setting and there was no sign of Rick or the car she had heard anywhere. Lacey had to think quickly. She made her way to the kitchen and opened a couple of drawers and found old ketchup packets and napkins, nothing of use. She made her way to the den which her mother had once used as her sewing room. Lacey was overwhelmed by emotion as she picked through the various material and unfinished garments. She came to a table where one item brought tears instantly to her eyes. It was a patchwork quilt. Lacey and her mother had worked on it three years ago. Jason had surprised both Lacey and Linda with a piece of fabric that he had a printer imprint various pictures of them together that Jason had taken over the years. Lacey and her mom had taken different pictures from the cloth and sewn them on a patchwork quilt. It was going to be their ongoing summer project. Lacey stared down at the unfinished quilt lost in a moment of anguish. As the tears rolled

DAD'S ADVICE
A SHORT STORY BY TAMMEAKA GRAHAM

down her cheeks the sound of a car door closing jerked her back into reality. Rick was back. Lacey scanned the room looking everywhere for something to defend herself. She caught a glimpse of something metallic in her mother's old sewing basket. Her mom's sewing shears! Lacey grabbed them and hid under the sewing desk. She prayed to an unseen God that she would make it out of there alive.

Taylor Preston felt like he was on top of the world as he slammed the door to his four runner. He would finally have his revenge. Lacey was so naïve and trusting. It had been so very simple. If only he had acted better the last time he and Lacey were together. She was being so juvenile. He needed her to trust him completely. It would have been easier to get her away from her father. "Damn him," Taylor swore out loud. Jason had made Taylor have to move up his plans. Lacey wouldn't even speak to him after that night and anytime she went anywhere Jason was there to drop her off or pick her up. Too bad he didn't the night Lacey was on her way to Donna's house. Taylor had heard about the study party and knew that Lacey wouldn't miss it. He had watched from across the street as the guests arrived at Donna's house. He had not expected to see Lacey walking toward the house alone. This was his chance. He had crept across the street and pulled Lacey into the bushes next to Donna's house. The chloroform had silenced any screams that Lacey may have tried to make. He carried her limp body to his car and was gone before anyone saw anything. He had not expected her to wake up in the car so soon. She started screaming and yelling. Stupid girl ended up getting the car door slammed on her ankle trying to fight him when he pulled over at the dirt road that led to the Manor. He bet it

Dad's Advice
A Short Story by Tammeaka Graham

was broken. If it wasn't, it was going to hurt like hell when she woke up.   He ended up having to dose her again with the chloroform. She was going to be in a whole lot more pain before the night was over. He would see to that after he got a chance to rest. He was tired from dumping Tonya's body. Tonya had said she loved him but then she betrayed him, threatened to go to the police when she found out about his plans for Lacey. That stupid bitch deserved what she got. It's too bad. That girl was a looker. She got it easy compared to what he had in store for Lacey. He walked up the drive way and let himself into the house. Thirsty, he walked into the kitchen, opened the fridge and grabbed a soda. As he reached into the cabinet for a glass he knocked the soda over. "Damn it!" he yelled. Rick grabbed some paper towels to clean up the spill but as he bent down to mop up the mess on the floor he noticed the cellar door was slightly ajar. He knew he had locked that door before he left. He silently crept to the door and slowly inched it open. Despite his best efforts the door creaked loudly. He walked slowly down the stairs knowing without seeing that Lacey would not be there. He smiled to himself as he felt adrenalin start to pump through his body, the hunt was on and he loved it.

Lacey crept along the hallway wall that led to the living room and kitchen with the sewing shears in hand. She stopped as she heard Rick in the kitchen moving around. Lacey flattened herself against the hallway wall not daring to breathe for fear of being discovered. She glanced around the corner just barely able to see Rick reaching for the cupboard door and watched silently as he started to clean up whatever it was he had spilled on the floor. He stopped suddenly and then she saw him walk to

DAD'S ADVICE
A SHORT STORY BY TAMMEAKA GRAHAM

the cellar door and go down the stairs. Lacey moved as quickly and as quietly as she could to the cellar door. She made it to the door just as Rick turned around grinning from ear to ear, the shock at seeing Lacey at the door quickly wiped the grin from his face. He raced up the stairs to the door. Lacey screamed and then jammed the sewing shears into Rick's shoulder and shoved with all her might. Rick's face contorted in a mixture of pain and surprise as he fell backwards down the flight of stairs. Lacey slammed the door, shut and locked it. She turned to grab a chair from the table to put against the door but as she spun around her feet slipped on the soda Rick had spilled on the floor and her legs went out from under her. She screamed as she fell to the floor, her weight falling entirely on her injured ankle. The sound of her anklebone completely breaking was like a gun going off in her head. Her ankle was broken for sure now. The pain was excruciating. "Owww!!" she cried out in agony. Lacey fought through the pain and made it to her feet forcing the chair under the doorknob of the cellar door. Her movements was much slower now, the pain in her ankle blurred her vision. "God, please help me. Please," Lacey sobbed. She was once again using the wall to brace herself but the walk from the kitchen to the front door was an open space with nothing to lean on. Lacey carefully edged herself off of the wall, tears streaming down her face. She felt herself falling and grabbed the sofa for support. The sound of something slamming up against the cellar door caused Lacey to jump. Oh, God she thought to herself. He was coming. Lacey tried to move faster but her ankle would not support anymore weight. She held on to the sofa gathering her strength. Slowly she let go of the couch again. Once again she heard the something slam into the cellar door, this time she could

Dad's Advice
A Short Story by Tammeaka Graham

hear the wood splintering. She felt herself falling to the floor just as the cellar door gave way. Rick was out and he was headed straight for her. The pain was unbearable. Lacey cried out for help but was met with the sight of Rick towering over her before she slipped into blissful unconsciousness.

Jason came to a screeching stop at the Manor entrance. The iron gate had been chained shut. He would have to make it on foot now. He grabbed his shotgun from the back seat. He had set it there just in case he really had to give Marcus a scare at the pool hall. He was glad he had brought it. He carefully worked his way around the gate until he found a spot where the trees were close enough that he could climb them and make it over the fence. Once on the other side Jason wove his way through the underbrush, careful to stay hidden in the woods that led to the house. As he approached the house he could see lights on in the living room. He ducked down and crept to the window that looked into the kitchen. The curtains were drawn blocking his sight but the window pane did very little to stop the sound that chilled his blood and stopped his breath. Lacey was screaming for help. Jason's blood was boiling. He had to get to his Lacey. The screams stopped abruptly. The silence was worse than the screaming. Jason crept around to one of the living room windows where one of the curtains was partially open. The sight that met his eyes drove fear into his heart and anger into his soul. Taylor was straddling what seemed to be a lifeless Lacey. He was gathering her up into his arms and carrying her toward the staircase. Jason watched until Taylor was out of sight. He stepped back and looked toward the upstairs window praying that Taylor switched on one of the lights. He needed to know what room Lacey

DAD'S ADVICE
A SHORT STORY BY TAMMEAKA GRAHAM

was in so that he could plan his entrance. The light in the master bedroom came on and Jason could see the silhouette of Taylor and Lacey.   The light went out and Jason crept back to the living room window. Taylor descended to the first floor and went down the hall and out of Jason's sight. As Taylor turned to go down the hall Jason spotted blood seeping from Taylor's shoulder.   He was hurt. Jason hoped that would work to his advantage. Jason quietly made his way to the front door, careful to stay low so he would not be seen by Taylor through any of the windows. He carefully tried the door. It was unlocked! Taylor had taken the seclusion of the manor for granted and left the door unlocked. Jason slowly eased the door open. Helping restore the Manor had benefits that Jason would have never thought would be an advantage now. He carefully crept into the house, avoiding the first two floorboards as he knew they creaked loudly when any weight was put on them. He carefully closed the door behind him, holding the door knob until the door was closed fully before allowing it to turn back in place. Jason knew that the bathroom in the back of the Manor held all the first aid items. Hopefully Taylor would be back there for a while. The amount of blood on his shirt looked like he was hurt pretty good.   Jason slowly ascended the stairs, careful once again to skip a couple of the steps that he knew would creak and give him away. Once on the landing he slowly crept to the master bedroom. The door was ajar and he could see Lacey sprawled atop the bed. He crept to the bed and sat by her side. "Lacey." Jason whispered softly. Lacey did not stir. Her breathing was shallow, her face ashen. Jason could not see any wounds on her and sighed in relief until he noticed the angle and which her left foot was bent. The bone was just barely visible through a small cut in her

Dad's Advice
A Short Story by Tammeaka Graham

skin. He didn't have to be a doctor to tell that Lacey's ankle was broken and it was bad. Damn it! Jason thought to himself. He was going to have to carry Lacey out of the house and down the road. How was he going to do that without Taylor finding them?

"Daddy?" Lacey called out in a weak voice.

"Yes baby, I'm here" Jason answered.

"It hurts daddy." Lacey sobbed

"I know honey. I'm going to get you out of here," Jason said softly.

"Dad, it's Rick" Lacey said, her voice trembling.

"I know. His name is not Rick, honey," Jason said, gathering Lacey into his arms.

"What?" Lacey asked confused as Jason picked Lacy up.

"Yeah, his name is ..." Jason was cut short as Lacey began to scream. Jason whirled around just as the blow to his head caused him and Lacey to go crashing to the floor.

"Taylor," Taylor finished stepping over the now unconscious Jason. "My name is Taylor."

Jason awakened to the sound of waves lapping. The sun had set. How long had he been out? He sat up, his head violently throbbing. Where was he? Where was Lacey? Jason thought as he jumped to his feet. The room swayed in front of him, his vision blurred. Jason felt sick to his stomach.

"Glad you could join us," said a voice.

"What? Who? Taylor!" Jason spat out angrily.

"Where is Lacey?"

"Daddy. Oh Daddy," came Lacey's sobbing voice.

"Daddy, daddy, wah wah" Taylor said mimicking a whining child.

DAD'S ADVICE
A SHORT STORY BY TAMMEAKA GRAHAM

Jason's vision began to clear. He could barely make out the boat house doors in the dark. Taylor had Lacey seated in front of him. She seemed out of it.

"What did you do to her? Jason yelled taking a step toward Taylor.

"Ah, Ah, Ah," Taylor warned as he pulled Jason's shot gun out from behind him and held it to Lacey's head. "You stay right there daddy," Taylor said smiling smugly. Jason stopped mid step; his eyes ablaze with anger.

"All of this Taylor? All of this because Lacey would not have sleep with you" Jason asked insidiously.

"No, you miserable sack of shit!" Taylor spat out. "I am going to tell you a story. A story about a little boy. He was his mothers pride and joy, she doted on him constantly. His father was a drunk so his mother was all he had. Well one night the little boy's mother decided that she had enough of her husband beating on her and decided to send the little boy to a friends house to spend the night. While the little boy was gone mommy waited until daddy fell asleep and poured gasoline all over the house and lit the match. She stayed long enough to make sure that she got a couple of burns so the police did not suspect anything but the little boy had come home from his friends house and saw everything and was trapped in the garage and got burned very badly in the fire." Taylor had a look of sadness in his eyes as he told the story. "Do you know who that little boy was?" he asked Lacey. Lacey mumbled a response. Taylor screamed "Wake up you little bitch! I asked you a question!" He kicked Lacey as hard as he could on her broken ankle. Lacey screamed. Jason tried to run to Lacey but again Taylor raised the gun to her head. "He was me! My mother never came back. She left me in the smoke and rubble and did not even come back for me!" Jason shuddered at

DAD'S ADVICE
A SHORT STORY BY TAMMEAKA GRAHAM

what he knew was coming next. Taylor grabbed Lacey by the hair and sneered into her face "Do you know who my mother was?" Lacey knew. She knew the moment she stared into his eyes. The picture in the cellar was of her mother and Taylor. Linda Fitzpatrick was Taylor's mother. Taylor was her brother. "Yes princess. I can see in your eyes that you know the truth." Taylor said. "You and your precious daddy were way more important to my mother than me. She never came looking for me. I looked for her. I found her too. When I saw my mother again I made her remember me. She called out to me as I dragged her into that lake. The cold water waking her up from her drug induced sleep. She said she recognized my eyes. I got her to the middle of the lake and pulled her under. She was so weak she couldn't fight. She found out how it was when no one came when you screamed. She knew my pain and now you will too." Taylor said directing his gaze at Jason. "You will know how it feels to live without the person you love more than anything in this world. Lacey is all you have left and you will pay for taking my mother from me," Taylor yelled dragging Lacey up out of the chair.

"No!" Jason called out. Taylor turned to him, "She didn't know" Jason said flatly. "Linda did not know. The police told her that they pulled a child out of the rubble and he was not breathing. She did not know you were alive. Your father had promised to kill her and you and she thought he had succeeded. Your grandfather had raised your father up to believe the a woman needed to be controlled even if it met beating her. They had always suspected Linda but could never prove it. They told her you were dead. Your grandparents were taking care of all of the arrangements. She never knew. She loved you Taylor. She loved you and you killed her!" Jason

DAD'S ADVICE
A SHORT STORY BY TAMMEAKA GRAHAM

screamed, tears streaming down his cheeks. Taylor kept the shot gun at Lacey's head. "You're a liar. My grandparents were liars too. That's why I had to leave them at the bottom of the lake. My mother was going to join them but you stopped that. Well, Lacey will end up there. Just the way our mother should have. Isn't that right, Lacey?" Taylor asked. Lacey was incoherent. Her face was pale and withdrawn. Jason had a sick feeling in the pit of his stomach.

"You switched Linda's pills that night. Didn't you?" Jason asked Taylor. Taylor responded with a laugh as he released Lacey to reach into his pocket. "You mean these pills right here? The ones Lacey is loaded up with? Yep that was me. Pretty good wasn't it. Thought the police would have locked you up for overdosing your wife but they are so stupid they didn't even check it out. They blamed it on the pharmacy." Taylor said laughing maniacally. He dragged Lacey out of the boat house to the edge of the dock. Jason followed behind, keeping his distance from Taylor as he still had the shot gun pointed at Lacey's head. "Time to go for a swim, Lacey," Taylor said flatly. As Taylor lowered the gun to push Lacey in Jason ran full speed toward him. Taylor, anticipating Jason's move, shoved Lacey in. Lacey sunk to the bottom. Jason slammed all of his weight into Taylor, knocking both himself and Taylor to the floor. Jason felt the wind being knocked out of him as Taylor drove his knee into his stomach as they fell. He rolled off of Taylor gasping for air. Taylor was up and kicking Jason in the rib cage before Jason could catch his breath. Jason spotted the shot gun lying on the edge of the dock to this left. As Taylor continued to kick him he inched closer and closer to the gun. It was just within his reach when Taylor suddenly spotted the weapon and kicked it down off the

DAD'S ADVICE
A SHORT STORY BY TAMMEAKA GRAHAM

dock. It landed in the sand, just missing the water below. Taylor raised his foot to kick Jason again but Jason managed to grab Taylor's foot and twisted it completely to the side causing Taylor to fall backwards, his head slamming into the wood on the dock knocking him out. Jason arose and walked slowly over to Taylor a dark stain was appearing under his head as blood seeped from a gaping wound in the back of his head. Jason regained him self long enough to remember Lacey in the water. He ran to the edge of the dock and peered into the water the light from the moon illuminating the surface Lacey was no where in sight.   "Lacey?" Jason called out. "Lacey!" He called again. There was no answer. Jason knew that Lacey had been drugged before Taylor had thrown her in the water. She had been under for a while. There was no way she would have survived being under for that long. His mind was no longer clouded or confused. He was going to kill Taylor. He had lost everything. Taylor had taken his life away and he was going to return the favor. Jason turned away from the water, fury blazing in his soul. He was stopped short by a sharp pain in his chest. Taylor stood before him, his eyes glistening with hatred in the moonlight. Jason slowly fell to his knees, his hands around the knife in his chest, blood spilling through his fingers. He could barely breathe. Jason struggled to his feet. He would not die kneeling in front of this bastard. He would never bow before the man that took the life of his beloved wife Linda or his beautiful daughter Lacey. He stood with his head high looking Taylor fully in his face. Taylor smiled smugly. "Now you see how it is to lose everything" Taylor said to Jason. Jason smiled and began to laugh uncontrollably. Tears streaming down his face. Taylor stared at Jason a bewildered look upon his face. "No." Jason said smiling. "It is you who will see how it

Dad's Advice
A Short Story by Tammeaka Graham

truly feels to lose everything." Jason said looking past Taylor. Taylor spun around just in time for the shotgun blast to hit him fully in his chest. A look of utter surprise crossed his face as the smoke cleared and Lacey came into full view. Shotgun held expertly in front of her. Her gaze fixed on him as he hit the ground. Slowly she hobbled to where he lay. Tears streaming down her face, she looked down at Taylor. "You killed my mother and tried to kill my father and me, but unlike you I have no hatred in my heart. My father always told me to love your enemies. Love those who hate you as hard as you can. I love you Taylor and I forgive you. I pray the Lord up above does the same." Lacey leaned down and closed Taylor's eyelids as he shuddered and drew his last breath. Jason watched his daughter, stunned by her words. He would have killed Taylor if he could have but not out of self defense but out of a need for revenge. Lacey killed Taylor to protect him. His words of love and compassion had taken root in her heart. Jason smiled and the love for his daughter showed like a light upon his face. Thank you Lord, he thought to himself, for letting him know that Lacey would be ok. Jason called out to Lacey and as she made her way to his side the darkness encompassed him and he faded away.

DAD'S ADVICE
A SHORT STORY BY TAMMEAKA GRAHAM

TOUGH LOVE
A SHORT STORY BY D. BROCKMAN SR

DBROCKMAN PUBLISHING PRESENTS:

TOUGH LOVE

A SHORT STORY BY: DBROCKMAN SR

TOUGH LOVE
A SHORT STORY BY D. BROCKMAN SR

Love…it's a death defying word that comes with a consequence each time the phrase, *"I Love You,"* is released and roles off the tongue. I once had the opportunity to encounter love at its purest form. I'm not sure how the encounter affected my life, but I do know that the situation that took place opened my eyes towards the way I feel when I hear someone say *"I Love You"*.

The year is nineteen hundred and eighty-seven; Ronald Regan was still in the office, Michael Dukakis was running against George Bush Sr. for president, floor model TV's were hot commodities, Kool Mo D, LL Cool J and Run D MC ruled Hip Hop while Queen Latifa and MC Lyte were trying to stop self-destruction. There was a form of destruction going on in South Florida in a city called West Palm Beach.

West Palm Beach is a very wealthy city, even back in eighty-seven before *City Place*, the *Nude Beach* across the bridge where the Triumph Estate is visible. West Palm Beach was a great place to visit. Aside from the city lights and the celebrities there were real people with real problems.

TOUGH LOVE
A SHORT STORY BY D. BROCKMAN SR

There was a family by the name of Klepklipt. The Klepkilpts' were originally from Miami, where they established a stable life for over seventeen years. The family never wished for anything and while growing up the kids had everything any kid could ever want, including parental love. The family was very close, and by the time the sun set each member let every other member in the house know they loved them. But the influence of alcohol and drugs scratched the surface and tore through the family of four when their oldest son realized he had an addiction. The family packed their things in an attempt to put their seventeen and fourteen year old sons in a better atmosphere. And that's where this story began...

7:45am mid July the year 1987, the morning started exactly like every other morning has started for the past seventeen years. The family had their ritual breakfast at 6:45am, at 7:10am the family starts preparing themselves to leave but everyday at 7:45am the family greets and says they love each other. The phrase "I Love You" was a very common phrase in the Klepkilpts' household. At an early age Mr. & Mrs. Klepklipt taught their two boys the importance of love. They also taught

TOUGH LOVE
A SHORT STORY BY D. BROCKMAN SR

them that whenever they use the phrase "I Love You" to make sure they mean it. They took their parents words and never used the phrase in vain.

On this particular day Mr. & Mrs. Klepklipt planned a trip to Miami to see some old friends. This was the first time in two years that they had visited Miami since their son almost wrecked their family love with drugs. Their nineteen year old (Raspen) had been clean for the past two years and he had been the inspiration in his sixteen-year-old little brother's (Jaquel) life.

Raspen and Jaquel drove their parents to PBI (Palm Beach International Airport) to connect with their 9:30am flight. Their parents were skeptical of leaving Raspen to look over his brother being that he was a recovering drug and alcohol abuser that once tried to commit suicide. They knew, however, that they spent a lot of money for therapy. Plus, he was in one of the best rehab facilities that money could ever buy. An old lady once made a statement about her addiction to cigarettes. She said she quit smoking for seventeen years and the urge to smoke was still almost unbearable to fight. Such was Raspen's delima.

For two years Raspen was clean, he made a promise to his parents that he would never use drugs or

TOUGH LOVE
A SHORT STORY BY D. BROCKMAN SR

alcohol again. He also made a promise that he would be a positive role model to his brother, Jaquel. He knew he couldn't bear to face his family if slipped back into that abusive life of drugs and alcohol.

These thoughts were filtering in both Raspen and his parent's minds as they gave each other hugs just before loading the plane. As Raspen and Jaquel walked through the airport they walked past a guy that stood six foot with an athletic build. They guy was wearing an all black, linen suit with a small chain around his neck. The guy stared at Raspen and winked as if he knew him. Raspen stopped to take a good look at him but he couldn't place the face from anywhere.

Raspen's mind started to saunter as he started thinking about the faces he met when he was using drugs. Those thoughts began to merge with the thoughts of the people he met in the rehab. He began to look around the airport and every face he saw looked like a familiar face. He started to perspire heavily. He looked over to his brother and he could see the concern look on Jaquel's face. Raspen made a dash for the restroom.

Jaquel remember how his brother reacted when he was using drugs. He remembered seeing his brother

TOUGH LOVE
A SHORT STORY BY D. BROCKMAN SR

breaking out into sweat after he had a fix. Even after the treatments, the therapy and the rehab there were many nights Jaquel would have to rock his older brother to sleep because he was still fighting his addiction.

Meanwhile, Raspen was in the restroom splashing water on his face. He was trying to get it together before his younger brother came running in to check up on him. But to his surprise that never happened. He quickly dried his face and rushed out the restroom to make sure his little brother was ok. When he made it out the restroom he saw Jaquel standing with his back toward the restroom watching the guy in the linen suit walk away.

"Jaquel." Raspen yelled from across the airport.

Jaquel turned swiftly as if he had just got caught doing something wrong.

"Were you talking to that guy? Who is he?" Raspen asked.

Jaquel replied, "No I was, I was just...yeah I was just admiring that nice suit he was wearing."

Raspen was no fool, but he had complete trust in his younger brother andhe knew he would never do anything-foolish being he had hands on experience as to what a wrong decision could do.

Tough Love
A Short Story by D. Brockman Sr

"Jaquel there is no need to admire what he is wearing, our parents are filthy rich. There is not much we can't have." Raspen looked at him with a grin on his face. "Now let's go to the Palm Beach Mall and buy anything we want."

"How about we make it the Palm Beach Garden Mall, that way we could pick up some rich girls. It's the summer plus we have the house for the next two days. You know what that mean!"

"We can parrrr-tay!" is what they chanted as they walked out of the airport.

They hit up both malls, met a couple girls and made plans to hook up with them later that night.

That night they hit up a local strip club off of Military Trail. No strip club would allow a sixteen year old to enter their club, but money talks. Raspen went to V.I.P. with one of the girls he met at the mall while Jaquel paid for lap dances on the floor. When Raspen came out of V.I.P., he saw the guy from the airport again. He dropped his head to gather himself making sure he didn't have a retake from earlier.

"Baby, are you O.K?" The girl asked with concern. He didn't answer. "Did I put it on you like that, you can't

TOUGH LOVE
A SHORT STORY BY D. BROCKMAN SR

even walk straight?" He smiles as she placed her hand on the side of his face and whispered in his ear, "I told you this Kitty-Kat even tame dogs." They both laughed as they walked toward Jaquel.

"Lil' bro you enjoying yourself?" Raspen asked.

"Look at this, I have a girl on both shoulders telling me what they're going to do to me when they get me alone." He replied!

"Sorry to burst your bubble, but we have to leave. There are a lot of things that we have to tomorrow. We'll have to pick this up tomorrow night."

"Well ladies you heard my big bro, we will be back tomorrow to pick up where we left off."

When they made it home, they took out two guns from their fathers' gun cabinet. They never loaded the guns (shells were in the cabinet) for safety reasons. Raspen pulled out a 12-gauge shotgun, and Jaquel took out a 9mm. They started cleaning the guns, which was a way they would pass time. After they took the guns completely apart, cleaned them and put them back together they called it quits and went to bed. Neither Raspen nor Jaquel put their gun back into the cabinet. Raspen placed his gun on the floor beside the sofa. Jaquel

TOUGH LOVE
A SHORT STORY BY D. BROCKMAN SR

placed his gun on the end table beside the lamp. They both went to their rooms to rest for the night.

Jaquel was awakened an hour later by loud moaning. The first thing that went through his head was that Raspen had a girl in the room. He jumped up and ran down the hall to get a peep, but he only saw his bother lying in the bed balled up like he was in pain. That was the same way his brother looked when he was using drugs. Jaquel was sure his brother was still clean though, so he went downstairs and slept on the sofa.

Early that morning Raspen awoke around 6:00am and made breakfast. Even though his parents weren't there, they still had a ritual to uphold.

Raspen woke his brother at 6:30am and told him to meet him at the table at 6:45am. 6:45am sharp they were eating breakfast. They made small talk until 7:10am. Jaquel went up stairs to take a shower to start his day. 7:40am Jaquel made it back down stairs and Raspen was waiting for him... holding a crack pipe in his hand! As soon as Jaquel saw it he stopped in his tracks.

"Raspen, what are you doing with that in your hand?" Jaquel asked. Raspen didn't answer he just looked at Jaquel with tears in his eyes.

TOUGH LOVE
A SHORT STORY BY D. BROCKMAN SR

A vision of the guy from the airport came to Raspen, he knew the guy from the rehab. The guy would always come around the rehab and sell drugs to the weak souls while they were trying to heel their wounds. He knew everyone in the rehab either had money or had a connection to get money. He never fell victim to what the dealer was trying to do. He knew his family was more important than the quick fix he would get from a high.

"That's what you were doing at the airport! You were buying drugs from that guy, and that's why you were acting strange when I called your name!" Raspen said with pain in his voice.

"What are you talking about Raspen? I saw you lying in your bed in pain last night look like you had a fix last night." Jaquel replied.

"I didn't even sleep in my room! I fell asleep in the guess room Jaquel!"

"No, I saw you lying in your bed balled up."

"You were hallucinating!"

"You're the reason Raspen, I wanted to feel your pains. I didn't want to get addicted, I just wanted to see what you were going through."

TOUGH LOVE
A SHORT STORY BY D. BROCKMAN SR

"Fool, you had a real life lesson! You saw all the things I went through, like how I tried to kill myself, and you go pull a stunt like this???"

Raspen picked up the 9mm from the table pointed it at Jaquel as he stated, "I will not let you destroy this family!" He was just bluffing. He wasn't going to shoot Jaquel, plus Raspen knew Jaquel knew the gun wasn't loaded. He put the 9mm down and picked up the 12-guage and he said, "I told you if I ever caught you using drugs that I'd take this 12-guage and blow you away!"

Jaquel reached out to his bother and said tauntingly, "I know there's no bullets in the gun, but you still don't have the nerve to pull the trigger."

Jaquel could see the frustration in Raspen as he bit his lip vigorously. Raspen thought he would give Jaquel a good scare to show him how it feels to be living on the edge. The clock began to ding letting them know it was 7:45am and that was the time they told everyone in the house they loved them.

With tears in his eyes Jaquel mumbled, "I love you Raspen."

TOUGH LOVE
A SHORT STORY BY D. BROCKMAN SR

Raspen replied, "I love you too Jaquel." And those were the last words Jaquel heard just before the gunpowder exploded and filled his chest with lead...

When the police and the detective arrive on the scene Raspen was too hysterical to speak to anyone. "*I love you, love you...*" is the only thing Raspen would say. Some say he kept repeating, "I love you..." because the last time he used the phrase he really didn't mean it. The detective found a note on the floor beside the fireplace and it read:

Raspen,

If you're reading this, I'm either dead or critically hurt. One day while I was at Wells Recreational Gym a guy walked up to me and he told me he thought I was you. He was a drug dealer, and he told me that he sold drugs to you. I didn't want you to go through all of that pain again by yourself so I started using drugs so we could have the experience together. You are my greatest inspiration and I never planned for this to happen. Yesterday when we were at the airport, I told the guy I was going to quit. He

Tough Love
A Short Story by D. Brockman Sr

then told me you never bought from him, only the other people in the rehab bought drugs from him. He told me if I stopped buying his drugs he would destroy our family once again. Last night I got high for the last time. I loaded the 12-guage and tried to commit suicide, but I couldn't bring myself to pull the trigger. Plus, I figure if I get someone else to do it I would still have a shot at heaven. I saw how distraught mom and dad were when you were on drugs and I didn't want to take them through that again. I remembered you telling me if you caught me doing drugs you were going to pull out the 12-guage and put me out of my misery. I hope you succeeded. Tell mom and dad thanks for everything, let them know I love them. Raspen, please don't be mad at me. I did this for us, and there is one thing I want you to always remember.

"I Love You!"

Lil Bro, Jaquel K.

Room 212
A Short Story by Bob Cain

DBROCKMAN PUBLISHING PRESENTS:

ROOM 212

A SHORT STORY BY: BOB CAIN

ROOM 212
A SHORT STORY BY BOB CAIN

When Officer Karl 'Chip' Zimmermann and his wife Maggie went to sleep at night, they slept soundly. Ten years ago, when he was seventeen and a junior in high school, his dad told him 'no', he was too young to get married ... especially to anyone 'like her'. But he loved her, and after the trial ended, he married her that summer before the start of his senior year. He took his savings for college and virtually everyone from school pitched to help. All their friends went to the wedding, then showed up again in December when baby Jay came home. Virtually everyone was there . . . everyone except dad.

Things slowed after graduation as both soon realized that with each other's love came unparalleled strength to endure any hardship; and through this strength they found a love that was timeless and forevermore. She, the good wife and mother; he, the good husband and provider – Both believed that, as long as they had each other, nothing bad could come their way.

But things inevitably change; and oftentimes more than not, even at the edge of sunlight, where shadows patiently play a waiting game, the past schemes in the darkness to push everything aside.

When the 'letter' arrived, Maggie immediately put it unopened in the kitchen cupboard and slammed the door. The next morning, after Chip left for work, she drank a cup of coffee, gathered her strength, tore open the letter, read it and wept. Mr. Jake Spaulding, No. 14576358, her old boyfriend and convicted murderer, was being released from prison, and it was necessary to inform her and others who may be of interest that he might be returning to town. She put the letter back in the cupboard, got Jay off to school, cleaned a little, went shopping and waited.

After dinner, when Jay was in his room, she told Chip about the letter, but he already knew. "I got it today

ROOM 212
A SHORT STORY BY BOB CAIN

... at work and I was wondering how I was gonna let you know," he said. Then, as they both started to clear the dinner table, he stopped suddenly and looked into her eyes. "You know it's strange . . . but I've been thinking about Matt most of the day, too," he said sort of sadly.

She thought quickly . . . "Yeah. Oh go on, get outta here. Go see Jay, he's waiting for you. Don't you know ten-year-olds have some like very great and serious fractions and decimals to figure out? I'm sure you can help. I can take care of cleaning up in here."

He gave her a quick kiss. Heck, he didn't need to be told twice. While Maggie cleared the dishes, he helped Jake with his homework. Then as a treat they played a little catch until sunset; and after Jay was asleep, they got ready for bed.

Maggie pressed her cheek into his chest and shivered. "I hope Jake doesn't come back to town. Please tell me you don't think he'll come back after of us do you?"

"Aw, Mag, you know I always watch out for us. And we have our friends to count on. If it gets too tough around here, you and Jay can leave town or you could always stay with some one."

"Yeah, I know . . . or we *could* always ask your dad if we could stay with him."

"We could . . . but if Jake's here, he'll be a target, too."

For a moment Chip thought about the sad story that was dad. When Matt was five and he was two, mom died from cancer and dad stepped in and tried to raise them the best he could. But dad always fixated on Matt "The Jock", *they both did,* but Dad did more. It was inevitable when Matt was murdered during his second year of college that dad lost control and started drinking. Almost overnight, riddled with shame and guilt, dad

ROOM 212
A SHORT STORY BY BOB CAIN

sought comfort – Southern Comfort -- and it was much easier to drink and forget Matt than it was to not drink, to remember he was gone, and to realize all that was left were the sports trophies in his room and the 'disobedient son with the tramp and the kid'.

"We're okay, even in spite of dad." He didn't want to talk about dad.

"I saw him Friday," Maggie yawned.

"Was he drunk, as usual?"

"A little. You know dad." Her voice went grave as the gravity of sleep began to take hold. "When I saw him I asked him if he got a letter and he said 'yes', just 'yes' and walked away. Thought he might say something about Jake but he didn't. I walked beside him and I sort of hoped he would take me up on my offer and come by for dinner, or something, but . . . (yawn) he didn't."

Chip yawned, too. "If only he just didn't drink so much," he said, his voice drifting a little. "At least you tried. I love you honey," he said as he kissed her again and rolled over to turn off to light.

"Me, too" she whispered as she began a silent prayer.

"Thank You, God, for giving me my precious family to love and nurture. Help Karl stay safe when he is away at work, and help Jay with his mathematics at school. I ask that you give me strength to share your precious love with everyone I meet. Heavenly Father, watch over us tonight. Amen."

It was almost midnight.

- - - - -

Jake's bus arrived in town at midnight. It was the last bus of the evening, and when he got off, with his cardboard box tied like a suitcase under his arm, he was thirsty and headed for Voelker's Bar that was near. It was

ROOM 212
A SHORT STORY BY BOB CAIN

Saturday night and the place was packed and young people were hanging outside.

He went inside and ordered a Jack and a beer, searching for familiar faces in the darkness. As his eyes adjusted, he saw one. It was an old man with a weathered brow, a crusty hand wrapped around a beer. Slowly he moved closer and closer to get a better look. Yes, it was him; and for the next two hours, Jake waited and drank the old man in. Jake was like a cat that had cornered an unsuspecting prey, and he could wait. *Oh God how he could wait.* What luck he thought as his order of steak and fries arrived. When he looked at the plate a small smile washed over his perched lips. What luck.

It was two a.m. when Voelker's let out and anyone left standing remembered where they lived and went there. On what was an unusually warm September night, when concrete still held the heat of the day, Mr. Zimmermann weaved through the alleyway to the back of the bar where he often went to sleep it off. There was a glider there he used when he was too tired to walk all the way down Market to the end of the street by the woods. A light fog whirled beneath an old streetlight as a few dried leaves, like schizophrenic mice, ran by his shoes and disappeared into the darkness. He laid down, took a deep breath, breathed out a heavy sigh, and was just about to fall asleep when he heard someone coming around the corner.

"Hey! Who's there?" he asked.

"Just another drunk, that's all Old Man. Do you mind if I sit a spell, I think I'm gonna be a little sick."

"Well, if you are, go over there on the other side of the streetlight behind the dumpster. That's where everyone goes because it's downwind from here. Hey, wait a minute . . . didn't I see you inside? You look familiar.

ROOM 212
A SHORT STORY BY BOB CAIN

Come 'ere so I can see you … my eyes aren't like they used to be."

As Jake walked closer he pulled out the cheap steak knife no one saw him pocket during dinner and he held it hidden by his side.

"I-I know you. Y-You're Jake, the bastard who killed my boy. I heard you were getting out. Some of us were warned that you might be around." He saw a flashing glint of steel as the blade of the steak knife cut into his face. It was too fast and as he moved to defend himself, the blade swung in an arc that left a huge gash in the side of his throat. In horror, he fell to the ground and reached up to try to stop the bleeding that would not stop. "They'll know you were here," he gasped.

As the Old Man held his throat, Jake jumped him plunged the blade into his heart so deeply and violently that the handle broke off in his hand. Soon it was over.

"Cheap steel," he said, sorrowfully, as he dragged the body over to the dumpster. He took most of the trash out, wrapped the body in some discarded plastic he found, put the body in the bottom of the dumpster and covered it with old trash. "Yeah, they might know I was here, but by the time they find your body, I'll be gone, old man. And so will your other poor excuse for a son, too."

The bar always left a garden hose out for quick clean-ups, and he grabbed it to wash off. Acting quickly, he remembered to steal everything in the wallet, and the little gold ring the old man always wore. He wanted it to look like a robbery if the body was found. But as luck would have it, he also found a key marked "Calcutta 17" which he knew to be to the old 'Calcutta Hilton', a small dirt-bag row of efficiency shacks where unfortunates went when they failed to move up and gave up.

ROOM 212
A SHORT STORY BY BOB CAIN

Knowing the neighborhood so well, by 3:30 Jake slipped silently unnoticed into the old man's shack. "Not bad," he walked around and stopped to admire himself in the bathroom mirror. He put his arm above his head and lunged forward.   "Oh no Mommy, look . . . it's, it's . . . Jake the Ripper."

He laughed as he pealed off his wet clothes, took a hot shower and walked dripping naked to the kitchen. He laughed as he opened the refrigerator and found a case of Coors. "Jackpot," he said, cracking one open and taking a long drink. "Look at you, Jake my man" he said proudly as he laughed out loud again. "Only one day out of prison and you've already gone and found yourself one fine little piece of property here."

If one were to ask him, he would have said that old man Zimmermann owed him at least this much for all those years he spent in prison. If he'd never gone to prison, he would have had the opportunity to have a lot more than just this. He would have been a better friend to Maggie, they would have settled down to raise a family, and everything would have been all *happydays-meets-pleasantville*. But after he killed Matt, it changed. She didn't like him after that . . . nope, not at all. As a matter of fact . . . Maggie became Chip's bitch during the trial, didn't she? Then all they wanted was to see him convicted and put away.

Sure, she told the truth and nothing but the truth when she stood up in the courtroom and said he wasn't with her on that Saturday afternoon eleven years ago when Matt died. Then she told everyone about how he and she had an abusive relationship, how on that day they had a fight, he hit her and she got a black eye. It was a hot afternoon, and after the fight Jake said he, Matt and Chip were going to the reservoir to swim for a while like

Room 212
A Short Story by Bob Cain

they always did. A couple of hours later, when the police came and asked her where he was, at first she told them Jake had just left to get cigarettes. But later, as the facts became known, Magpie said a lot more than that, didn't she. . . *didn't she* . . . "that chirping little bitch."

Jake reached in the kitchen drawer for a large butcher knife and held it up by the kitchen window. Its clean silver surface beamed in the dawn light and there was something about his reflection in the blade being so poetically right he smiled.

Maggie could be a real bitch whenever she wanted to be, that's for sure. He remembered the last words she said to him after he was sentenced and was being walked out of courtroom. She clung to Chip's arm and yelled, "You're dead to me, Jake. It's OVER, we're THROUGH! You HEAR me!? You LOST it all . . . you lost everything!"

"Yeah. Well everything *this* you fucking cunt," he said as he sliced into the counter top. "And fuck Chip," he said as he hacked away a piece of the wooden window frame. "You both were fucking around behind my back, I just know it." He took a drink of beer. "Heh, but do I have a surprise for both you," he said as he hacked chunks out of everything he could hack on his way to the living room.

Exhausted, he sat in old man Zimmermann's LayZboy knockoff and flipped through the phone book. "Let's see now . . . I wonder where those happy little Zimmermann's live, anyway? Ah yes ... why there you are."

Jake took the day off and sat around Calcutta 17, and as far as he heard no one had found the body behind Voelker's yet. What a great idea it had been to take the time to bury it deep. It could get pretty rank back there.

ROOM 212
A SHORT STORY BY BOB CAIN

Early Monday morning his phone call to the city confirmed that a truck came on Tuesday to pick up the trash. If he was lucky, he had time to plan his next move.

Later Monday morning, after most of the locals were off to work, he left The Calcutta to take a walk through the woods back toward town. They called it the Hobo Woods and the name stuck. Actual transients moved through them like a virus during the summer, and no one knew what he might catch if he went in there often enough.

It was a beautiful, sunny, breezy Monday, and rain clouds were just starting to gather. The sound of creaking trees and dead leaf rattle made just the right cover for any noise he might make as he walked along. Suddenly, in the distance he heard the radio playing old songs. Under a shaded canopy, he moved closer and saw something he hadn't seen for over ten years. Two women were hanging their wet laundry on gray cotton clotheslines and then lifting it high into the air with old wooden poles to dry.

"I just love these blustery days," Thelma said as she hoisted her white sheets to the wind.

"Hanging yer sails, Matey?" Mildred asked in her best brogue. "Argh me Bucko, where would ye like to go?"

"Inside, with dry sheets I hope. Heard there's a storm coming and I'd rather not pay for those dryers that don't dry if I can help it. She fluffed the sheets by hand to get some of the wrinkles out. "Rain needs to stay away for about an hour and they'll be dry by then." Thelma turned the radio up a little to listen to *Mona Lisa.*

"I just love that song," Mildred said as she grabbed another handful of clothespins. "And that song, Unforgettable, that Natalie did with him is so nice, too."

Thelma was a little we from handling the sheets and she shivered. "Yeah. Hey Mil, what did you think

ROOM 212
A SHORT STORY BY BOB CAIN

about that dancer being killed in the apartments early Sunday morning? Wasn't that something?"

"Yes. I heard she broke into Room 324 and was killed by that nice quiet guy, you know, the one in the wheelchair that lives under you and Leo. Oh, Thelma, just imagine if she had decided to break in to where you guys are?"

The thought of that happening made Thelma shiver even more. "H-hey, not to change the subject but I heard Jake was being released from prison and there is a possibility that he might be coming back to the area. I mean I've been out there for the past week telling everyone to let me know if they see him so I can let Chip and Maggie know. I also told the teacher at the school so she can watch out for Jay, too, but she told me they already knew. What reason does he have to come back here anyway? There isn't anything here for him any more. When I was at Janie's Salon, her daughter Gloria's boyfriend's mother Rita who works as a secretary at the station got a copy of the letter and as far as anyone knows, his mom and dad booked for the West Coast after the trial and they never wrote to him."

"Really? What a shame," Mildred said.

"When he was growing up his dad did everything for that boy. Took him to the games, bought him the best sports stuff. He was such a nice kid."

Millie was shocked. "Nice?! Well Rita said that he had a record from the time he was sixteen, thieving and fighting. He was even in juvenile detention for two months when he was fifteen for selling pot outside Voelker's. She said it appeared like there was a history of violence or something. I just don't get it."

"It was the father that was the problem," Thelma said as she turned the radio down. "I remember now. He

ROOM 212
A SHORT STORY BY BOB CAIN

pushed Jake too hard to make varsity, and all he ever wanted was for him to go pro. And that's how it happened."

"What happened?"

"That murder, silly." Thelma said as she turned the radio completely off for effect. "They say Jake killed Mike because he was better than him at sports. Yes. Let's see now . . . from what I remember, he, Mike and Chip were up at the reservoir practicing for a swim meet and, as Chip tells it, Jake and Mike made a bet to see who could hold his breathe longer underwater -- you know, like all kids do. Well, they both went under and Mike stayed under. To hear Chip tell it, his brother's body floated lifeless to the surface, and when they dragged it to the shore, his throat had been cut."

"Jake."

"Yep. At first he denied everything. The water was dark and there were no witnesses to the crime. He dropped the knife and hoped it would never be found, but it was. The cuts on Mike's throat were caused by the steak knife he used. Later, Jake broke down in court and cried and told everyone how he hated Mike for being better than him in everything he did. His dad used to say to him "Why aren't you like Mike?" so he only kept Mike around because he gave him something to strive for."

"Shame."

"Yep. I was there at the trial. I saw it all. When Maggie screamed at him that they were through, as he left the courtroom he turned around and looked at her and Chip and said, 'I should have killed both of you when I had the chance.'"

And I will. And I will. He thought as he moved back into the woods. *Fucking Busybodies. Didn't they know they weren't supposed to talk trash about people who*

Room 212
A Short Story by Bob Cain

weren't there to defend themselves even when they really were there to defend themselves? He smiled. *But at least they took it. . . outside.* He heard himself laugh out loud. *I know, I'll just go around the long way to Voelker's. After all, the sight of the former murderer, Mr. Jake Spaulding, stepping out of the woods right now in the flesh would probably give the old hags a coronary.* He smiled again. *Yeah, and they'd make doodoo in their Depends. I mean like 'shit' man no one wants to see that.* Jake laughed a little.

"Did you hear that?" Thelma said.

"Hear what?" Mildred asked, cocking her ear to one side. Thelma yelled out. "Hey, you kids know you aren't supposed to be playing in those woods. There are bad people in there and you could get yourself killed playing in there." She waited and listened; they both listened. But all they could hear was the sound of the leaves as the wind blew through them.

"What did think you heard?"

"Oh it's gone now. But, but just for a moment, Mil, I thought I heard someone laughing."

Jake entered Voelker's at around 1:00. It was pretty much empty, with just four ladies by the Juke Box having burgers and fries, and two firemen and a policeman at the bar. Merle Haggard was playing something pretty and pretty Miss Kimmie was behind the bar with the owner, Voelk.

When he walked up to the bar, Voelk and the policeman immediately recognized him. The policeman sat still and decided to let Voelk do all the talking. He hadn't broken any laws so why not.

"See your back."

ROOM 212
A SHORT STORY BY BOB CAIN

"Yep, got some pulled pork and fries for an old friend, Voelk?"

"Sure, have a seat, but if you can help it, try not to rile up the ladies over there. They're lesbians and they come in all the time. Just fair warning."

"And a beer?"

"Coming right up."

During lunch Voelk pumped him for information about prison, and about some of the other kids who he knew ended up there. Just idle talk, nothing much. Jake was downright charming and honey-dripped from his lips. "You know, Voelk, I saw the light in prison. I got me some religion, I gave up my bad ways, and praise jesus I went and got myself born again. In fact, every night before I went to bed, I prayed that Maggie, Chip and Mr. Zimmermann could find some way in their heart to forgive me. I was crazy and my dad didn't help none," he said as he took a drink of beer.

Voelk stopped washing the plate and looked up. "I know he came down on you pretty hard all the time. You know that's something a young man in college shouldn't have to bear.

"That's the way I see it, too, Pops. Guess the board did too, because they let me out with ten more years to serve. Hey, I found Chip and Maggie's address in the phonebook and it says they are over at the apartments in Room 212. I tried to call them, but no one was home."

The policeman spoke up. "Chip's up at the reservoir with the Scout Troop. They're going for their swimming badges. I think Maggie's there, too, with Jay. Want a ride, I'm going that way?"

And as Jake said thanks and started to leave, two ladies were slow dancing to 'gee aint it good to be back home" playing on the jukebox.

ROOM 212
A SHORT STORY BY BOB CAIN

The police car rolled off of Market Street and started up the long path that led to the swimmers. Jay asked the cop to stop for a moment so he could take a piss. When the car stopped, he pulled out one of old man Zimmerman's steak knives and drove it neatly into the officer's temple. The officer didn't even see it coming.

Meanwhile, in town, Ms. Kimmie discovered something rather horrible in the dumpster out back. Just as Voelk called the station to let them know the bad news, Jake crouched low and ran cautiously up the embankment. Quickly he pre-positioned himself to remain unobserved behind one of the above-ground holding tanks. *Made it! Now let's see what Chip is wearing today.* Good. Just as he hoped, Chip was not wearing his gun. *W-What! Was he, crazy? Didn't he know there was a homicidal maniac on the loose? Oh my, was this ever going to be easy.*

Jake remained unobserved by the tank and fence as he watched a few remaining Scouts qualify. When they finished, Chip gave them their badges and they ran right past him laughing down the hillside and back to their happy little homes to show their badges to their happy little daddies. Jay ran toward the gate and turned to his dad.

"Sure, go on. We'll meet you at home," Chip said.

"When you get there, make yourself a sandwich and we'll be there soon," Maggie yelled after Jay.

As soon as Jay turned out of sight on the path below, Jake made his move. As the security gate was shut behind him, Maggie turned and screamed.

"Screaming aint gonna help you, ba-a-a-by," he sang. Chip spied the knife and grabbed both towels and

Room 212
A Short Story by Bob Cain

wrapped them around his hands. "Get over in that corner and stay there," he gestured to Maggie.

"But there's two of us ... we can take him," she said bravely.

"Listen, I'll take care of this."

"FUCK YOU BOTH AND LISTEN UP. First, I'm going to cut you up Chip. Then, after that I think I'll fucking take you out in the woods, Magpie and fuck you till I hear you squawk." As he came closer, Maggie moved to the other corner.

He realized that she might be able to make a break for it if he rushed Chip and he went back to the gate, picked up the lock and key and locked it. "Think you're fucking smart, bitch? Well you aint."

"Wait," Chip said. "Jake, let's talk about this. You haven't done anything wrong yet. Let's get you some help."

The walkie talkie blared. "Chip? Chip, are you there? This is Rita at the station. I just heard from Thelma that someone found your dad dead in the dumpster behind Voelker's. Chip can you hear me? We think it was Jake. We think he's coming for you."

Chip reached down and picked up the Walkie Talkie. "I hear you, Rita. He's here with us now at the reservoir. He has a knife."

Suddenly Jake ran at Chip, Chip countered to get out of the way, and Jake turned it on him and pushed him into the fence. Chip turned around as Jake deftly slid the knife into his upper left bicep and gave it a masochistic twist to pop a couple of veins. As Chip leaned over and saw his alizarin crimson blood dripping from his elbow, he wondered what other things Jake studied while he was at prison.

ROOM 212
A SHORT STORY BY BOB CAIN

Jake couldn't believe how good the vendetta felt. He had waited a long time for this moment and damn it if he wasn't going to have a little fun. "Christ, man, don't they teach you how to defend yourself in police school?" he asked sarcastically. "At this rate, you'll be dead in a couple of minutes."

Chip stood up and ran at him with all his strength. "They taught me plenty," he yelled. But Jake was quick and although Chip managed to land a hard right-hander upside his head, Chip took a wound in his other hand as he protected his ribcage.

Jake tasted his own blood as it trickled from his cheek. "You fight like a fuckin' girl. You sure aint your brother," he chewed.

"Wait a second, wait a second," Chip begged. "This isn't getting us any where."

"Shut up and fight you coward."

Maggie watched in horror as Jake sprang at Chip for the third time. Jake took another powerful blow to the face this time, but everything was in slow motion as the knife, which appeared to hang motionless in space for a moment, flew from Jake's left hand to his right and he masterfully drove it deep into the back of Chip's left calf.

Chip ripped a towel from his bleeding hand and grabbed the hand with the knife. As he tried to wrestle the blade free, Jake pulled it out sharply. Then as he stood up, he sliced a seven-inch gash across Chip's chest, Chip fell and Jake started his move in for the kill.

Maggie screamed. "Wait, Jake, please don't kill him. It doesn't have to be this way. I still love you. I'll go with you if you let him live. I have the keys to the car over there. Let's go, let's just leave."

"Leave and miss all this fun? What are you, bitch, are you crazy?" He jumped on Chip, they rolled toward

ROOM 212
A SHORT STORY BY BOB CAIN

the water's edge and he stabbed him in the ribcage. The pain was excruciating. Chip managed to wrap his legs around Jake and for a moment he appeared to have the upper-hand. Chip broke a couple of Jake's fingers and was just about to butt heads with him when Jake reached down and found the walkie talkie. He used it like a brick against Chip's head and managed to break free.

"Listen Jake, Jay is your son!" Maggie screamed

"What the hell are you fuckin' talking about?" He asked. "What do you *mean* he's my son?"

"It's true. When you were charged, I didn't know what to do. I thought I was pregnant but I didn't have time to tell you and you didn't have time to listen. You were all into your sports shit. After I found out, I tried to tell you but you were pissed off and hit me. Then you killed Mike and I knew you were guilty when they charged you. I couldn't tell a soul. I went to Chip and he said that he would help me keep my secret. He told me that he always loved me, even when I was with you, and I saw this as an opportunity to have the kid and get ahead. Sorry, Chip. At first I thought I'd just use him and move on, but after a time, I don't know what happened. I guess I just sort of fell for him, you know, like a puppy brought in from the streets falls for a kind hand, warm meal and a nice place to sleep."

"You fucked me over. Don't think I forgot."

"Yeah, but he's your boy, Jake. Didn't you get a good look at him when he left? He's strong and he'll go far. He is already first in track and he's first squad in midget league."

Chip was listening and he couldn't believe it. What was she doing? Was Maggie selling him out? No, it had to be something else. He spoke up.

Coincidentally Mishappened
The Anthology

Room 212
A Short Story by Bob Cain

"Listen up, Jake. It's true, when we were first married Maggie told me the baby was Matt's baby and that you killed him because he had sex with her and you found out. I figured the least I could do was take care of my dead brother's kid. But one year after the baby was born, she told me that the reason she named the boy Jay was so he could sort of be named after you."

"So what's your point, dead man?" Jake growled.

"Well the point is that every day from the time he was one until now all I've done is ride him and hit him and treat him like he IS you, Jake. Even if you kill me, I've more than made up for it by the way I treated him. He'll never recover. He's pathetic. It was so easy, that little piece of shit even looks like you! Same eyes, same build . . . I swear sometimes I hurt him so bad that finally he stopped crying. For awhile there all I had to do was threaten him and he would pee all over himself like a scared little puppy."

"DIE!!!" Jake screamed as he rushed forward and they both fell to the ground. Jake stabbed him in the leg as blood sprayed into his eyes. He wiped his brow, and as he grabbed Chip's arm, the knife suddenly slipped from his bloody hand.

At that moment, Chip grabbed his arm and hurled him into the air. When his head hit the cement edge of the reservoir there was a loud crack, and for a few seconds he was disoriented. This was exactly the moment Maggie was waiting for. She ran forward and kicked him repeatedly in the head as Chip grabbed the knife and stabbed him repeatedly in the throat.

When they stepped back, Jake crawled to his knees and gazed at Maggie with steel-gray eyes. Didn't she know how much he had thought about her in prison? Didn't she care that he still loved her and all he thought about

ROOM 212
A SHORT STORY BY BOB CAIN

was to touch her one more time? He grabbed Maggie's ankle when he fell forward. She stood there helplessly as she felt life flow out of his trembling fingers. Screaming, she watched in horror as Chip reached down and pulled the dead arm away. Jake was nothing now, must less than he had been before he came out of his hole. Chip held her close as he reflected on how different things could have been.

There was only one question, though, one incident that could never quite be explained. No one knew for sure, and even though she denied it later, it was believed that Rita made the call. For as they both looked in the distance on that fateful afternoon, Thelma, and literally everyone else in town, was coming up the hill.

ROOM 212

A SHORT STORY BY BOB CAIN

THE WRAP UP

A SHORT STORY BY: THE PUBLISHER

COINCIDENTALLY MISHAPPENED
THE ANTHOLOGY

THE WRAP UP!
A SHORT STORY BY THE PUBLISHER

Over the itinerary of my years on earth I have learned that people penetrate our lives for diverse reasons, and sporadically they may only stay for a few seasons. The story that's about to be told is a bouquet of untruthfulness that has been compiled to compose a factual statement. Arthur J Harding told me that as a writer, one would use lies to fabricate the truth and "Make shit up to make it sound interesting." Those were his precise words. Today I'm going to take a stand and give an informal, undisclosed statement on how a writer thinks. I will embellish upon the idea of literary creativity after this phenomenal story is told.

Recently in a city that was just off the Gulf of Bay lived a guy who had prior lives that sequentially followed him through two decades. The more he ran the heavier his tribulations became, so one day in that city off the Bay his running came to a halt. He knew when he stopped running his life would never be the same again, plus he knew he would have an extensive debt that he owed to society! I know I'm blabbering, *Let The Story Began!!!!!!!!!!!*

THE WRAP UP!
A SHORT STORY BY THE PUBLISHER

Beginning of the 80's – Mid Eighties

If anyone remembers anything about the Nineteen Eighties they would tell you about Donkey Kong, Pac Man, Atari 2600, what went on in Mr. Roger's Neighborhood, Donnie Simpson on B.E.T., Jeri Curls and even acid washed jeans. However, I saw the eighties from a different perspective. If you were born between 1980 and 1989 you know that "Eighties Babies" could possibility have either heroin and/or cocaine running through your veins. Cocaine was top seller, and made it's contribution to the lives of every person that was willing to make a purchase.

In the early eighties I grew up on a little camp called South Shore. Everyone there was like family. There had to be over 50 duplexes in the camp, and they ranged from one bedroom to three bedrooms. In some situations the camp owner would knock down the wall that divided the duplex to make it into an uniplex←(That's an author's word). My family was one of the fortunate to have the luxury of living in one of those apartments.

The camp had two sides. One side of the camp was for migrant workers that migrated from state to state for work, then there was the other side in which I grew up; it

THE WRAP UP!
A SHORT STORY BY THE PUBLISHER

was for seasonal workers like my parents. The seasonal workers worked mostly year round, harvesting any crop that was in season at that time. All my childhood I watched my parents work just about everyday, planning a flourishing life for me. That was all taken away from me one day at the age of thirteen. I can remember that day just like it was yesterday. I was an eighth grader in middle school at Lake Shore, the old one.

It all started one day while I was having lunch. I was always a quiet person and most of the time I ate lunch alone. I had friends at school but they didn't take the same lunch as I did. I pick up my pint of chocolate milk off of my lunch tray the swig that would finish it off. Just as I brought the milk carton to my lip I could smell the imitation Nestle Quick that had settled in the bottom. As soon as the milk touched my lips, a wintry chill overcame my body. For several seconds I couldn't hear anything that went on in the world. It was like time bunged the moment so I could receive a message that was undeliverable because my mind was too young to accept it.

After my precious moment passed and my life was reset to normal, everything was happening fast. The

THE WRAP UP!
A SHORT STORY BY THE PUBLISHER

chocolate milk I was drinking found my esophagus, blocking my breathing path. Pure instinct caused me to spit the milk across the table. When I opened my eyes from the output I saw milk dripping from the guy across the table. The guy looked like he was pissed, but I think he was going to take it as a loss until he let the girl next to him put jumper cables on him. Plus, the guy sitting on the other side of him started feeding him battery acid by telling him that he should hit me in the head with his tray. I had never been a violent person in my life, but that day I had an out of body experience and I knew my whole life had just changed. The moment seemed to be frozen by time!

I stood up from the table and I could hear the kids in the cafeteria oooing! When they noticed I was standing with intentions, their ooo's turned to ooh's! I reached down and picked up my tray, and without thinking I smashed the guy in the face with it. Mind you, it was not the guy that I spit the milk on but the guy that was hyping him by telling him to hit me with the tray! After he dropped to the floor I smacked the girl in the face for instigating! As she fell to the floor the guy behind me stood up asking me what the hell was I doing? I assumed my

THE WRAP UP!
A SHORT STORY BY THE PUBLISHER

chair bump into him making him spill food and he was pissed too! So before I would give him the chance to retaliate I hit him in the back of the head with the tray. Keep in mind this was the eighties and the trays were made out of fiberglass not plastic.

After I saw him fall to the floor I saw the teacher racing across the cafeteria with rage in eyes and intentions in their steps. As one of the teachers approached me reality must've checked him when he saw the three people picking themselves off the floor. He stopped in his tracks because he knew I was a BEAST with that tray. As he got closer I drew back with the tray still in my hand, and then I heard a voice say *"watch out!"* I turned to see who was trying to alert me and I locked eyes with the guy that I spit milk all over. That was the last thing I saw before I saw the little white stars followed by darkness!

I awoke about an hour or two later, surrounded by nurses and two policemen. My head was throbbing with excruciating pain. I could barely open my eyes, and when I did my vision was blurry. I could hear the nurse speaking to me but my mind was still sending messages to my brain

The Wrap Up!
A Short Story by The Publisher

informing me that my vision was ambiguous and my hearing was still impaired.

While he was waving his hand back and forth in front of my face one of the officers asked, "Son, can you hear me?" It looked like his had the glow like Bruce Leroy, from that movie <u>The Last Dragon</u>. I wanted to ask him how he was doing that, and then my recollection returned and realized why the officers were there. I forced out an "Uh-huh", nodding my head yes with fear of what they may say next.

The nurse held up her hand and asked, "How many fingers am I holding up?" I really couldn't see her hand that well, but I knew from every other time someone asked me that question they always held up two fingers.

"Two" is what I said as I rubbed my eyes hoping it would help my vision!

"Do you remember what happened?" The nurse asked as she lowered her hand to her side.

I didn't answer the question, but the look of innocence I was giving must've given me away. I saw the two officers whispering to each other. I turned to the nurse as I saw her being escorted out of the room. I just

THE WRAP UP!
A SHORT STORY BY THE PUBLISHER

knew I was in big trouble. As soon as she left the room the Assistant Principal, Mr. Darville, walked in the room. He was a tall lanky guy who had to tilt his head to the side to enter the room.

He sat down beside me and he spoke with a low voice, but his tone was convincing and I knew to listen to what he was telling me. "Son, you know you done fucked up. But being the person that I am, plus the fact that I have never seen you in my office the entire time you've been at this school, I'm going to cut you a break. Instead of giving you ten days out of school, I'm going to give you the rest of the week off. Today is Wednesday, take the rest of the week to get yourself together and come back Monday with a new attitude. Those officers are going to escort you home."

I looked at him with guilt in my eyes, I know something was wrong with me but I didn't know what it was so I couldn't ask for help. I still had this sensational feeling that something out of the ordinary was about to happen but I couldn't quite put my finger on it! The office secretary gave me all the paper work I needed to notify my parents that I was being suspended and an explanation. I walked to the car with the officers and when they put me

THE WRAP UP!
A SHORT STORY BY THE PUBLISHER

in the back seat I felt violated. As they drove me home two ambulances passed us. One of the ambulances stopped about a mile a head were a car had flipped off the road and into a canal. They had the highway blocked so we had to take a dirt road that took about thirty minutes just to get back to the main road.

As we made it to the camp I could see the flashing lights from what I presumed to be the second ambulance. The closer we got I could see the ambulance was in front of our uniplex. My heart began to pound vigorously! It was heartrending to see my father was smashed underneath a car. They say he had just finished doing a break job on my mother's car, and he jacked his car up to fix something under it when the car fell off the jack and crushed him. Just as I tried to get myself together a detective drove up in an all black Chevy Caprice with tented windows. As he stepped out the car he shook his head. He walked over to the officer that I was with and whispered in his ear. The officer dropped his head as he turned to look at me. I could see pain in the officer's eyes as he tried to turn his attention away from me.

The detective walked over to me and sat me down on the porch. He apologized for the lost of my father, and

THE WRAP UP!
A SHORT STORY BY THE PUBLISHER

then he added insult to injury. He told me my mother was just involved in an accident and she had drowned. He explained that she lost control of the car she was driving and ran it into a canal.

I was breathless. I started to hyperventilate. My breathing path became so narrow that my body shut down and I fainted.

THE WRAP UP!
A SHORT STORY BY THE PUBLISHER

Mid 80's – Early 90's

After my parents passed, for the next few years my life took a drastic turn. I moved to Palm Beach with my aunt Tricia who had two older sons that she had been taking care of since her husband died in a shoot out in Rivera Beach over a big cocaine bust. Rivera Beach is called Raw-Vera for several reasons, but I won't disclose how it got that name. It was cool having the big brother figures around, it gave me something to look forward to each day. One of my cousins (Moocher) was much older, he was around twenty years old but he was still living with his mother. He picked up where his dad left off, but he was a little more careful and he kept the house protected. He ran a trap (A Drug House) on the other side of town so to him money was not an object. My aunt knew about it but he was paying all the bills so she never complained.

My other cousin (Muncher) was only a couple of years older than me, and we spent a lot of time together. We shot marbles, chased girls, we beat up a couple of people and we even got beat up by a couple of people. He was like my brother from another mother.

THE WRAP UP!
A SHORT STORY BY THE PUBLISHER

My aunt always told us to stay away from the drug spots because anything could happen at anytime and a bullet doesn't have a name on it. One day during the summer some kids from around the way said they were going to Gaines Park to a basketball tournament. They told us that a team from Orlando, Tampa, Jacksonville, and Belle Glade was going to be there. Muncher wasn't that interested in going, but I wanted to go see who was coming from the Belle Glade. I told Muncher that I was going to go, and he told me that we would have to get permission from his mother. I knew aunt Tricia wasn't going to give us the approval being that Gaines Park held a bad reputation and a lot of fights took place at that park.

I convinced Muncher to sneak to the park and told him we were only going to watch a few games and then we were going to come back home. He was still a little skeptical until I mentioned that there would be plenty of girls out there. I knew he had a weakness for women, and he gave in with out a doubt.

When we made it to the park we walked through the courts and I saw a team dressed in Maroon & Gold and their uniforms had PFP on it. I knew they were from

**THE WRAP UP!
A SHORT STORY BY THE PUBLISHER**

(The Muck) Belle Glade because I remember Robert Clark putting together a PFP Tournament when I lived in South Shore. PFP stood for Pure Funk Productions, letting you know they will go Pound For Pound. After watching them play their first game in that tournament I understood how they got their name.

Muncher wasn't that interested in watching the game, he was more interested in the girls that were walking around. After the game finished we walked around and started mingling with a group of girls. They were cheerleaders from the Jacksonville team. Every other word that came out of their mouth was Duval! They really loved their county. Then we saw two girls that were standing under some bleachers trying to get some shade.

Muncher, the woman go-getter he was, approached them with open conversation. As we conversed with them there were a couple of guys looking over towards our way. I saw them but I didn't pay them any attention. The girls told us they were from Tampa. We talked about fifteen minutes and Muncher leaned over and he whispered into the girl's ear. He then leaned over to me and said, "I shall return with another one to add to the list!" He smirked as the girl grasped him by the hand and they walked off. I felt

THE WRAP UP!
A SHORT STORY BY THE PUBLISHER

a little eerie watching him walk off with her but I knew he had intentions and he wasn't going to stop until he got them satisfied. As the one gorgeous redbone and I sat and talked I noticed the guys that were staring at us were walking around the building that Muncher and the girl were behind. I started asking the girl questions about her friend and the guys that were staring at us, but she pretend that she never even saw any guys.

I ran as fast as I could to get to Muncher with fear in my heart that he may be in danger. By the time I made it to the building I was tired, but what I saw propelled my adrenaline. The guys had Muncher surrounded and the girl was standing off to the side. It looked like Muncher had already given one of the boys a black eye and the other three were hesitant to run up on him.

I yelled, "Hey, what ya'll trying to do?" Muncher looked in my direction and one of the guys jumped on him. I ran towards the guy that was on Muncher's back, but before I could make it to him one of them fed me a knuckle sandwich. I staggered a little but when I saw Muncher getting the best of the guy that was on his back I knew this was going to be one of those good fights that we were going to talk about all the way back home. I turned

THE WRAP UP!
A SHORT STORY BY THE PUBLISHER

and hit the guy that hit me and he grabbed me. My father taught me that if some one ever gets up on you, you do what ever it takes to get them off of you. As I pierced his flesh with my semi-sharp teeth I saw the girls' laughter turn to a frown when they saw the blood.

Muncher was getting the best of two of the guys, the one I bit was on the ground screaming and the other guy was standing back as if he was scared to get bruised. I ran over to give Muncher a hand with one of the guys and I glanced into the girls' faces and I saw terror in their reaction as one of them screamed, "NO!!!!!!! NO!!!!!!!! DON'T SH..."

POW!!!!! The bullet pierced through my cousin's flesh and into his stomach. I turned to see where the shooting was coming from and I saw the guy with the gun pointing it at me!

POW!!!!! I hit the ground as the bullet burned through the flesh of my thigh. I could hear the girls screaming with fear in their voices. Nothing can replace that day. I saw my cousin lying on the ground. I was trying to get to him but the pain was horrendous. I saw

THE WRAP UP!
A SHORT STORY BY THE PUBLISHER

his body quaking like he was going into a convulsion. I reached out to touch him but I was too far away!

Some people came around the building that must've heard the shots, but by the time they made it there the guys were gone and so was my cousin. That was twice within five years I had lost three people that were dearly close to my heart. At that moment I started to **"Love not to Love!"**

THE WRAP UP!
A SHORT STORY BY THE PUBLISHER

"THE MISHAPPENED"

Over the next year I went from the little teenage boy that shot marbles and chased girls to serving cocaine and sleeping with grown women. I started hanging out with Moocher and my life was moving extremely fast, but as an eager teen in my adolescence I loved the rush. I found out why my aunt called my older cousin 'Moocher'. It means: a taker, a user, a stealer, and etc... He lived up to his name. Though he never physically took anything from anyone, he stole a lot of dreams with the transaction of a plastic bag.

I was deep into the game. I started out Nickel and Diming but I was eager to get rich fast so I can move out of Palm Beach and never return. I would sit out back of the drug rehabs and feed on the innocent prey that they were trying to rehabilitate. One day out of the blue I hooked up with my number one customer. It was a young guy I called Jay. His name was really strange like Jashen or Jaspen, so I called him Jay because I could remember that. His last name was even stranger, it was Klepkilpt. I saw him at Wells Park one day. At first I thought he was a guy that I saw in the rehab but I could tell that it was his

THE WRAP UP!
A SHORT STORY BY THE PUBLISHER

brother. I played it cool and told him that I was his brother's dealer, hoping he would never tell his brother.

I served Jay for less than a year. I saw him in the Palm Beach International Airport with his brother one day, and I threatened to tell his brother what he was doing if he stopped buying from me. A couple of days later while I was having breakfast I picked up the paper and it was front page of the Palm Beach Post..."*Young Klepkilpt shot by older brother. Suicide note found at the scene of the shooting!*" They titled the article "**Tough Love**!" At that moment I knew I had to change my way of thinking and I had to change several things in my life.

I gathered some of my belongings and I decided to move north. I moved to a small town in Pennsylvania called Belle Vernon. I lived there for about thirty days before it got to the point where I just couldn't take it anymore. The building that I was living in was called the Market Street Apartments, and to this day I still think that apartment building is haunted.

The very first night in the Market Street Apartments there was a murder. Some drunken dancer climbs the fire escape and forced her way into this crippled guy's apartment. His name was Calvin or Kevin, but I do

THE WRAP UP!
A SHORT STORY BY THE PUBLISHER

remember the girl that was shot. Her name was Monte Carlo, just like the car. If she'd climbed my fire escape I would have taken that Monte Carlo for a ride, know what I mean? She had a very nice figure and she was really pretty. She had to do something very extreme to have that guy shoot her, or maybe it had something to do with the evil that's stored in that building. I can still remember that night...it all took place in **"*Room 324*"**

One night while I was in Voelker's bar throwing back a couple of drinks and trying to cope with all the things that were going on in Market Street Apartments. While I was ordering my drinks a guy sat beside me by the name of Jake. He was looking for a couple that lived in **"*Room 212*"**. I remembered his name because it was the same as my favorite child hood wrestler, Jake the Snake! Jake had just been released from prison for murder. He looked like he was up to something mischievous, but who was I to judge? As he sat there I gave his story a chance, thinking he had learned his lesson. As soon as he got finished eating his food I saw him take the steak knife and slide it into his pocket. I knew at that moment he was up to some no good. Not even twenty-four hours later Jake had made Belle Vernon Top News.

THE WRAP UP!
A SHORT STORY BY THE PUBLISHER

Moments after Jake left I ordered a couple of more drinks and I tuned into an old couple that was at the Bar celebrating their upcoming unification in **"Room 423"**. They were talking about an incident that happened a few blocks over on 5th Ave. There was a little girl named Lacey who was dating a guy by the name of Rick, whose real name was Taylor. They say her father Jason tried to warn her about the guy, but she felt like she was old enough to make her own decisions and she didn't need her **"Dad's Advice"**! As they continued the story I found out the guy Taylor was really Lacey's late mother's lost son!

I went through some things in Florida, but after spending less than a month in Belle Vernon I learned to appreciate all the things that I was trying to run away from. I moved back to Florida in the summer of 2000. I hooked up with a guy by the name of Jamie. We chased women and spit poetry and verses over tracks he produced in Studio 21. It was a very sad event in early fall when Jamie's mother renounced her throne here on earth to sing in the heavenly choir. I saw how the pains touched Jamie. He even wrote a story about it entitled **"Death is only the Beginning"**!

The Wrap Up!
A Short Story by The Publisher

Three years later I met an angel on the bus by the name of **Stella-Mae** who was on her **Walk to Liberty**. She told me about her situation and how she did some things in her past that she wasn't proud of. She also told me a story about how she and one of her friends were hanging out in an abandoned building and a guy by the name of Sebastian was being chased by these two guys that she thought were drug dealers. That particular story opened my eyes and made me understand my **"Morals"**! I told her how distant I was from my past life, and I explained the things I'd done after I told her about a dream I had on **"A Typical Sunday"**!

THE WRAP UP!
A SHORT STORY BY THE PUBLISHER

"THE COINCIDENCE"

Coincidentally these stories are creations sprouted from the authors' perspective filtered through their thoughts and scattered on paper by a fine ink to gather the attention of the reader through events that Mishappened.

The truth behind this Anthology is much like all the stories. Each author has some sort of relationship with each other. For starters, each author worked together for a company called Syniverse Technologies. All of them knew of each other, but there were limited conversation amongst them.

"Dad's Advice" was written by T. Graham. Ms. Graham has a reverence for her father figure, and some would say it's a coincidence that she wrote her first short stories on the topic she chose. My thought? I would say that it was something that Mishappened.

Room 324, 212, & 423 were written by Bob Cain, and coincidentally he is from a small town in PA, called

COINCIDENTALLY MISHAPPENED
THE ANTHOLOGY

THE WRAP UP!
A SHORT STORY BY THE PUBLISHER

Belle Vernon. Even though Market Street Apartments are not real, the Mishappened events portrayed by him have made me hesitant about visiting the city of Belle Vernon.

Unfortunately there is no coincidence in the story "Death is only the Beginning", by Jamie Bush. That Mishappened event was a true story and he had to live through that.

Padget Williams story," Stella-Mae's Walk to Liberty", coincidentally came from a day that she and I were riding down the street and she saw a women that looked liked she'd just been through a Mishappened event. Also, it is very true that I met an Angel on the bus (Padget Williams) in 2003.

My stories, Dexter Brockman Sr., are also a coincidence. "Morals", "Loving to Not Love", "Tough Love", and "Typical Sunday", are direct reflections on me. I am from Palm Beach County and I've seen a lot of Mishappened events that have taken place. That why it's still strange that all these people, from all these different places, are connected to some sort of event that happened!

THE **W**RAP **U**P!
A **S**HORT **S**TORY **BY** **T**HE **P**UBLISHER

"The Promise"

I promised I would make an informal, undisclosed statement on how writers create. Some people would want to say a gift and a talent are the same thing. A talent is something acquired, something you get your hands on and you pick it up and run with it. You can learn to write poetry by listening to Jazz, Gospel, reading poetic books or what ever behooves you. In fact, you can become a very talented poetic writer using this method.   A gift, however, is something given to you and it's yours...FOREVER! When you run across a person that can sit and write poetry or just crank out short stories, even though they have never done it before much like the authors in this book, then you know that person has a gift. I said that to get to this...Most writers, gifted writers, take a lie and twist it to cover the true behind it! I'm not saying this is a factual statement for all writers, but most of them are too selfish to place their personal lives on Front Street. So Arthur J Harding, you were wrong! I can't tell you exactly how it works, but for writers, I guess you can say that's just something that   <u>COINCIDENTALLY MISHAPPENED!</u>

pg 151

Dexter Brockman Sr., *29, has been residing in Tampa, Florida since 1999. He is originally from South Bay/Belle Glade, Florida, located in the Western Palm Beach County. He's the fourth child of a family of six in which he has two inspiring big brothers, a loving sister and phenomenal parents that have supported him through th good, <u>and the bad!</u>*

Dexter Brockman Sr. found a love for writing at an early age. When he was 10 years old he wrote his first poem and he knew he had a gift. It took him a few years to exploit his gift, but he always knew he loved to write. After meeting an Angel, who happened to read some of his work in 2003, she told him that he was a writer. It was then that he believed his gift needed to be heard by the world. Two years after that statement he wrote his first novel (I'm In Love with not Loving Anyone) published in 2006 under his publishing company, <u>DBrockman Publishing</u>.

Mr. Brockman has a degree in Business. He also builds and repairs computers, writes and reads books in his spare time. Writing is his love! He is a father to his kids, he's a brother to his siblings, he's a son to his parents, he's a provider to his lover, he's a servant to his God and he's a writer to the world!

Jamie Bush, *27, year old leaf from Clearwater (Wick City) Florida traveling where ever life's majestic wind will blow him. He's just a young black male trying to find his way in life and serve his purpose to the fullest and change the world.*

Jamie learned he had the gift of writing when he was in college. One day he awoke and wrote some poetry, one became two, and from there a writer was born. Jamie doesn't write as much as he would like to, at times the fire that once burn in him for writing has died down. Sparks flare up every now and then so you never know.

Right now he's just chilling trying to turn cents into millions. It's stressful wanting to be somebody. But he'd rather die trying that live not. Don't correct that that's how he want it. But he thanks Dex for the many aggravating phone calls and emails about getting a short story in.

"Because I was gonna write a short sex story but, well you know...I didn't. But peace to all and remember... I'm an artist and I'm sensitive about my shit. Translations: 'If you don't like what I wrote then kill ya self' J/K...." says JBush

Padget Williams *Originally from Boston, MA.
Ms. Williams have been writing, and creating stories since
the age of 14.*

*She became interested in publishing her work while
attending the University of Massachusetts. While being in
such an eclectic environment, she was inspired to
write from variety of people she met and the many different
places she visited.*

*Ms. Williams is current working on a book
of short stories to be published in the near future.*

Mr. Robert "Bob" Raymond Cain, *54, married and a resident of Tampa, Florida since 1988. Bob has presented three short stories from his upcoming novel, "The Market Street Chronicles", in which they re-appear as part of a larger work. All he will say is that if you enjoy them, you might want to get the novel when it comes out early next year.*

Bob is an accomplished pianist, watercolorist, poet, dog-trainer and gourmet cook. He has spent a large portion of his life traveling and has been virtually everywhere. He is a highly decorated veteran of both Vietnam and Desert Storm, and he met his wife while working as a member of Sir Norman's staff at US CENTCOM. His life is a little slower now as he plays piano, does calligraphy for freaking-out bridezillas and their beaus, and occasionally he helps businesses and people port their telephone numbers in accordance with FCC regulations.

Bob's wife, Martha, is his heart's best friend. One could do a lot worse, but never better. He raises tri-color Pembroke Corgis and hopes to begin work soon on a companion book, "The Fifth Floor." He can be reached at rcain1952@verizon.net and enjoys emails.

THE ANTHOLOGY!
A DBROCKMAN PUBLISH

Tammeaka Graham *was born in Staten Island, New York on December 2nd, 1977. The oldest of 4 siblings she found she could disappear from the constant sibling rivalry into the fantastical world of reading. Charlotte's Web was the first book she read and she still loves it. From there her love for writing blossomed. First there was poetry and then stories. In high school Tammeaka read every fiction book in the library and never once considered it nerdy. She considered it an escape, something like a vacation from peer pressure and parental expectations.*

One of Tammeaka's fondest memories is of standing in her doorway with a pink piece of chalk in her hand at 4 years old waiting for her father to come home. No matter how tired he was he took his time to take her, his talkative little girl, to her room with a black board and show her how to write her ABC's. She fell in love with writing right then and there and it has been that way ever since.

Tammeaka hopes to impart that on her children so they too can know the joy of literature. Isaiah, Elijah and DeAnna Jane are the three best things God could have ever given to her that she never knew she needed. She and her children take Saturday trips to the public library, which are an adventure to them but for her they are keys to success. Her oldest son Isaiah is slowly falling in love with reading and it makes her heart burst to know that he will always have a memory of when he fell in love with literature as she has the memory of her pink piece of chalk. Elijah hated reading because he thought he was not very good at it but now that he has practiced and advanced 8 levels in a month's time he can't wait for Library Day. DeAnna (her youngest) thinks the best part of the library is sitting on the floor and playing with puzzles with the other children in the library. One day she hopes to introduce her to her all time favorite book as well even if it isn't Charlotte's Web!

Tammeaka graduated from Grace M. Davis High School and majored in Para Legal Studies with a minor in English at Humphrey's College in Modesto, CA. She currently resides in Sunny Florida and is looking forward to fulfilling her life long dream of writing her first novel.

www.ingramcontent.com/pod-product-compliance
Lightning Source LLC
Chambersburg PA
CBHW020334110726
47898CB00003B/879